"I think you're beautiful," she said simply.

She set her wine glass on the table and slid toward me. She took my hand, a hand that felt numb till the second she kissed my fingers one by one, her mouth touching like a dance. The gold and shadow edged across her face, and I reached around her neck to touch her hair, expecting a burn, knowing I'd been wanting to do this since the first time I saw her.

Barely a touch this kiss, like mouths whispering together. Her hands came to my face, pulling me closer till tongues curled and electric sparks flashed behind my eyes. I twined and twisted her hair, practically feeling the blazing red that was soft and wild and warm. She leaned away, the kiss smoothing the air.

Her eyes seemed so deep I could fall into them. She traced the edges of my lips and the curves of my cheekbones, touching like my face was a raised map and she a blind woman trying to find the shape of the land. I squeezed my eyes shut again as she brushed my neck with the tips of her fingers, throwing sparks that seemed to grow and pinwheel into my head from where they'd begun, leaving me half-frozen with the hot and cold of it . . .

THE
FINER
GRAIN

THE FINER GRAIN

Denise Ohio

NAIAD PRESS
1988

Printed in the United States of America
First Edition

Edited by Katherine V. Forrest
Cover design by Pat Tong and Bonnie Liss
    (Phoenix Graphics)
Typesetting by Sandi Stancil

Library of Congress Cataloging-in-Publication Data

Ohio, Denise, 1962—
    The finer grain / Denise Ohio.
        p.   cm.
    ISBN 0-941483-11-8 : $8.95
    I. Title.
PS3565.H58F5 1988   87-31190
813'.54--dc 19   CIP

About the Author

Denise Ohio was born in Santa Maria, California in 1962. She is a musician, filmmaker, poet and playwright as well as a novelist, and currently she is writing her second novel, *Blue,* and playing guitar in a rockabilly band. She makes her homes in Minneapolis, Minnesota, and London, England, and cannot for some reason stop getting into trouble.

For Miss Kitty

So what? This is what I think now: that the natural state of the sentient adult is a qualified unhappiness. I think also that in an adult the desire to be finer in grain than you are, "a constant striving" (as those people say who gain their bread by saying it) only adds to this unhappiness in the end — the end that comes to our youth and hope.

—*F. Scott Fitzgerald*

snapshots

Jessie's dead and the nightmare's back.

With a snap the match flared and burned, making my eyes water and hurt from the light. A headache got all red around the edges of my brain, trying to find a shape so it could gallop around. Damn heat. Damn dream. I flicked ash into a saucer on the edge of the coffee table. Jessie never kept an ashtray in the house since she didn't approve of smoking. She didn't approve of much — in fact she'd be having a fit if she could see me down here in her living room practically bare-assed naked in front of God and everybody.

The tacks that lined the upholstered chairs glittered like tiny brass moons. Leaning back on the couch, I inhaled all the way down, the smoke from the tip drifting off. Light shimmered off the curtain sheers, shining through the whole room, making the spidery crack across

3

the white ceiling look like an old lady's bumpy hand reaching for the front door with the waterstain as a thumb. Lately everything and everyone seems just like that, flat, and I'm just another picture no one can touch or get behind.

I went to a window and looked through the rust-smelling screen that turned everything into little framed pictures all the way down the street. No lights in any of the houses, not even the flickering of a TV set. Nothing but the crickets in the grass and me in a T-shirt Bobby Lee'd left that caught the light, too, turning almost blue with the full moon being so bright.

The first fresh air all week blew, making electric shocks dance under my skin. I wiped sweat off my forehead, thumb rubbing the crescent scar near my right eye. Jessie used to yell at me every time I touched or scratched or poked at it, even once told me to wear bangs so's no one could see it, but I never did. This scar doesn't bother me so much, not like the other. I rubbed my belly, tugging the skin of that one, the one that slices all the way down, hiding under Bobby's shirt.

The varnished wood smelled like pine trees as I ground the cigarette out on the sill. This house was mine to sell, trade, or burn to the ground. Now all I wanted was to get the hell out.

The carved wood of the china hutch seemed to be making faces at me and the dull greenish handles smiled, quietly asking to be pulled. I opened the top left cabinet and inside was the latest and the last bottle of Jessie's sherry. Feet slapping at the wood floor, I wandered back to the couch, bottle open before my ass hit the fabric.

Taking a drink that made my eyes stretch, I tossed the lid at the potted fern near the window. That plant was ugly, even in the dark, all scrawny and weedy like a wild thing growing out of the floor. Once I had a plant there named Arthur that Jess didn't mind, she even thought he was pretty when the late afternoon sun would slip into the room onto him until she caught me picking leaves off to dry in the oven. I think one of her church friends told her he wasn't exactly legal, so she killed him. I drank some more and had a goosebump attack that sent the last tingles of sleep scattering down my back.

I tried to tell Jess about the dream once. She said she didn't get it, said having a nightmare over and over was a sign of bad luck or a sick mind. I don't know which one she thought I had, but she sure thought she could cure it by praying.

I sank into the couch. The old lady's hand was still reaching and I watched so long I thought it was moving.

* * * * *

I got off the couch this morning with my arms and legs shaky from too many cigarettes and the sherry, and didn't stop for anything but a pair of cut-offs and a chocolate-frosted pop tart. Didn't matter if I slept in my clothes or wore the same thing for weeks; Daniel didn't care. The phone rang in the house just as the backs of my legs hit the hot vinyl seat of the Buick, almost like it was planned.

"Shit." I ran back inside. "Yeah, hello?" I panted into the phone. I was going to have to cut down to a pack a day or die of a heart attack by the time I was twenty-five.

"Amory Walker, please."

"This is me." The kitchen was dim after the bright sun, dark enough to hide everything stashed in the corners.

"This is Kendra Sites. Did I wake you?"

"No."

5

"I have some good news. This may be a bit premature, but it looks like we have a buyer for your house."

"I only called you last Friday."

"This is unusual, but we were trying to make things easier for you under the circumstances."

What a pile of buffalo chips. She wanted quick money just as much as I did.

"I was calling to arrange a showing," she went on.

"Pick your time," I said, wrapping the phone cord all the way up my leg, then letting it unwind and coil up around itself.

"Is eleven o'clock convenient for you?"

"That's fine."

"All right, then. I'll take care of everything. Thank you and goodbye."

"Good —" It didn't matter if I finished or not. She'd hung up on me already.

Hanging the phone on the hook, I looked around. All the dirty dishes fit fine in the cupboard with the dishsoap and the furniture polish, and the dining room was all right. The front room was a little lived-in looking, with shirts and shorts curled up like little cats all over the place. I stuffed everything into the coat closet under the stairs and as long as nobody opened it, nobody'd ever know I had to kick it all down to get the door shut. My bedroom was hopeless. The bathroom was clean since I'd been trained since babyhood to keep it that way.

Jessie's room was exactly the way she left it, orderly and neat, not even a stray shoe sticking out from under the bed. I should've packed her clothes on Saturday, after I'd picked out a dress for her to be buried in. I'd chosen the burgundy one that she bought for my graduation and never got to wear. It wasn't real fancy, but nicer than anything I'd seen her in. The mortuary guy looked at me like I was playing some kind of joke on him, as if Jessie had all kinds of expensive clothes I was planning to sell and I didn't want to waste a good dress by letting it be shoveled over with dirt. I could've bought her a new dress, but that one she picked out so she must have liked it and it seemed right that she wear something she wanted, not something I got out of the blue that she'd never seen.

It was almost ten. Daniel wouldn't mind if I took time off for errands since I opened and closed the store every day that he was gone and didn't get paid extra for it. Cranking the radio, I cruised over to Applee's Super Market to get some boxes.

Finishing a cigarette in the parking lot, I watched the bagboys haul groceries out to cars. Some of the bagboys weren't boys anymore. They were my age or older, working with their sleeves rolled up to their elbows, the T-shirts they wore underneath not enough to stop the half-circle of sweat under their arms.

At the check-out I asked Suzie Munson if there were any boxes I could have. She bobbed her head in some direction while looking at her nails and chewing gum like a cow. I knew her from high school, when she was a cheerleader. Back then she got pregnant and got an abortion. Everybody knew about it, even heard her boyfriend hadn't paid for it since he didn't know if it was his or not. I grabbed my boxes and shoved them in the back seat of the Buick, one inside another, and drove off, windows all the way down and radio blasting all the way up.

It was almost ten-thirty. They'd be there at eleven. How long did it take to show a house anyway?

The strange car in front of the house meant Kendra Sites was already there.

7

Jessie's is a nice house, two stories and a cellar all in a pretty brown color, not a beige or tan, with dark trim. I'd painted it myself and that trim had been a bitch, going all the way around the big windows on either side of the screened-in porch, two eaves from out of her room, and all the windows around to the back. The roof's too sharp to lean over, so I had to troop around the house with a ladder. Couldn't lift my head or my arms for days afterwards. There's still a spot where I knocked over the paint pan and the roller bounced all the way down, leaving splotches in the roofing. At first Jess was scared, then she got pissed; I had to stay up there and scrub till it was gone. By that time it was too dark to tell if I'd gotten it all and I was really hungry. Looking from this direction, I can still see the stains.

I turned around in the Cornfeld's driveway and drove Memorial Boulevard all the way around to waste time, past the high school with a Go Team sign tied to the fence, by the courthouse where there weren't any people just a lot of birds, to the west side. At the freight yards, storehouses rose off the street like blank tombstones, their grayness broken only by spray-painted names and hearts and true-love-4-evers. I took a left and headed for the bridge.

There's only one way over the river from this part of town and that's the Suicide Bridge. It was called Suicide Point for when the Indians used to make people jump off the cliff if they were in disgrace with the tribe. Take a flying leap from this side, bounce off the rocks a few times and land in the water. These days diving in from a safe distance would kill somebody, it's so full of trash. But someone came along and thought it would be a great place to put a bridge and while they were building it, one of the workers did a swan dive and missed the river completely.

8

They had to scrape him up with a shovel. A couple of years ago six kids from the high school tripped out on some weird shit and thought they could fly and now a lot of people won't come up here anymore because of that, like Tommy Balderson whose brother was one of them.

It was windy and I could smell the water soon as I pulled over. All that horse shit about West Virginia's rivers running clean is exactly that — horse shit, and they smell like it, too. Around here all of them are muddy and dirty-looking, even the ones that became environmental projects. This river flowed right out of Ohio already filled with coal dust from the mines and industrial crap from the factories, everything that could be thrown in. David Shaw once even found his car sinking into the gray water two miles upriver and Eagle's Peak when he forgot to set the emergency brake. He and Louann Ballas had been in the picnic pavilion and I bet it was quite a surprise to find out the splash wasn't their little piece of earth moving, but his daddy's Monte Carlo going for a swim.

* * * * *

I unlocked the bookshop, dragged the wire racks with the twenty-five cent paperbacks and the two lawn chairs out to the sidewalk. Re-counting the dimes, I heard someone come into the store. A girl, Straitsville Community College on the front of her shirt, the sleeves torn and going to loose strings like her cut-offs, was standing there. She had a little braid with a red band peeking from the right side of her neck.

"I was wondering if you have a copy of 'When You Are Old,' " she asked.

"Who wrote it?"

"William Butler Yeats. It's just one poem."

9

She said Yeats funny. I always thought Yeats rhymed with beets. "Well, I don't know," I said, stepping over to the shelf on the right marked Literature and squatting down. "It may be hard to find."

"I can look," she said, sitting on the floor to see the Y's better.

"Okay." She was going to get herself covered with crud down there.

"Hi, darling," a familiar voice came from inside the front door.

I met him at the desk. "Hi, Daniel."

He gave me his tight-lipped smile and a hug. A lot of people didn't like Daniel but he was my friend and I'd been working for him since last September, after graduation and summer were gone.

"How are you? Are you okay?"

I nodded. When I first told Jess about my new job, she knelt in the kitchen to ask the Lord to recognize that she'd done her best with me and when His judgment came, He was to remember I wasn't blood kin and a person could only do so much with bad genes. She was upset because Daniel's a Jew. God probably wasn't paying attention anyway; we'd both been hearing the same prayer since I was seven and pushed Bart MacElfresh off the swing so hard he fell flat on his face and busted his front tooth.

"I'm sorry I couldn't get back. I tried, but family obligations . . ." He trailed off, looking at the ground. "Hey," he said, stuffing his hand into his pocket and pulling out a wad of cash as big as my fist. "I have your money. I owe you for three weeks, right?"

Slipping six fifties out of the middle, Daniel held the bills out in a straight line from between his fingers. His hand was clean and the veins branched across the back

10

and disappeared around his knuckles. I took my money, shoving it into a pocket while he did the same with his.

"You've been doing a terrific job, Amory, I wanted to tell you that."

"Thanks, boss."

He suddenly held me at arm's length, staring into my face. "Look a little tired, though. Has Bobby Lee been bothering you?"

"Not any more, Daniel." When I told Bobby I was going to be working in the bookstore, he grunted and drank his beer. He didn't care what I did around Daniel Jacobson because the guy was queer as a three dollar bill, anybody could see that, he said. I asked how he knew and he said because Daniel acted more like a woman than a man. But Bobby thought every guy was a fairy if he didn't work in the mines or the factory, and besides, he thought he could beat us both into the ground if he heard we messed around. Bobby Lee Carling was half a foot taller at six-foot-two and an easy fifty pounds heavier, but Daniel wouldn't be as easy to beat on as he thought. He might not be built like a Coke machine with a head, but he's strong as a coiled-up rope.

"Excuse me?"

I'd forgotten the girl; she was carrying a book with its cover barely hanging on by the picture on the front.

"Oh, hi, I'm sorry." Daniel smiled at her.

"That's okay," she said, looking at me. "How much do you want for this book?"

"We usually —"

"Two bucks and it's yours," Daniel broke in.

"All right."

He took the book and stepped behind the desk. "Do you need a bag or anything?"

"No," she answered, untangling some bills and handing them over. "Thanks for your help," she said, smiling at me while Daniel tucked the money into the cashbox.

"No problem." He looked up to grin.

"Thanks for coming in," I managed to get out before she stepped through the door. She gave a small wave and disappeared into the sunshine.

"How about some breakfast?" Daniel asked.

"You just got here," I answered, turning to him. He'd let his beard grow further up his face. I liked it. The red in his hair made his eyes seem more black than brown.

"So?"

"I already had breakfast."

"I'm buying."

"You got yourself a date."

I closed up and Daniel locked the door. Instead of putting his keys back in his pocket, he kept throwing them up in the air to catch them, dropping the bunch twice by the time we got to Jake's, half a block away. We slid into a booth at the end of a long row of video games.

"Get anything you want," he said, shoving a menu over.

I picked it up. "Like it's going to break you, boss."

Sylvia rolled herself over to our table, giving us her full attention since we were the only ones in the place. Daniel asked for two beers and her eyebrows went up. Guess it wasn't every day that people came in to drink beer at eleven o'clock in the morning. He repeated himself and she waddled on back to get them. I think it was Bobby Lee who told me Sylvia'd once won some county fair beauty pageant, been pretty enough to even catch one of the Macon boys, but something happened and she went to hell in a sidecar. Couldn't tell she'd once been beautiful. It was all buried under sixty-pound saddle bags she carried on each hip and swaddled in her foot-high beehive hairdo. Old Sylvia was a gravitational miracle, every square inch of her poured into a stretch-as-you-grow waitress uniform with her name embroidered in red over her left tit.

With the dull, hollow sound of glass on formica-covered wood, she set the bottles between us. I lit my first cigarette and puffed like the world was going to end.

"You ready?" She stood over the table, listening as Daniel ordered for both of us. Sylvia never writes anything down, just stands there twisting her jewelry, first the ring with the big green stone that has to be fake, then the electro-plate gold bracelets jangling around each wrist, spinning them with hands looking like a pair of rubber gloves someone blew up for balloons.

The squeal of frying hamburgers sifted between the metal sounds of the radio as I peeled back the label of my bottle. When I was little I used to think flashy things like that were special, pretty, and I'd collect silver gum wrappers and other shiny things from off the street to keep in a cigar box till Jess found out and made me stop.

Daniel picked up the label to smooth the curved edges. "Why are you so quiet?"

I smashed out my cigarette. "Thinking."

"Aren't you even going to say welcome back?"

"Welcome back."

"Smartass."

"How was the trip?"

"The usual. Parents," he rolled his eyes. "Feel lucky you never had to deal with them."

Sylvia brought the food, mine in a little blue plastic basket and Daniel's in a red one. He poured ketchup on the wax paper surrounding his hamburger and started in.

13

I tried a bite, then gave up. It was too hot in here to eat anything, even the dill pickle wilting in the basket.

"Hey, Sylvia, may we get two more beers, please?" he called out between chews, too loud in such a small room.

She set her *True Confessions* down and nodded.

"So when are you leaving?"

I glanced up. He was wiping a string of ketchup off his beard with his fingers. "Leaving?"

"Yes, leaving."

"Who said I was?"

"You did, remember?"

"What are you talking about?"

Sylvia brought another round, taking my empty. Daniel had half of his left. Damn, I always could outdrink that boy.

"When you started at the shop —" He reached for a napkin to wipe his face. "You said you were going to be a writer."

"So?"

"Why aren't you eating?"

"I'm not hungry." The plastic upholstery felt greasy through my shirt, like someone had rubbed french fries across the back of the booth.

"I thought you wanted to go to school."

"Why should I? I don't need to learn grammar or margins or that junk. I'll have my editors take care of it." I gave him a big smile. He didn't buy it.

"Amory, there's a hell of a lot more to writing than margins." Daniel wadded up the one napkin and took another out of the holder.

Shit. He knew how much trouble I had my last year of school. The diploma was still in the envelope they mailed it in, behind the salt and pepper shakers on the kitchen table.

"I can't afford it."

"How much are you getting for the house?"

"Who'd let me in? I practically flunked out of high school."

"No, you didn't. You did fine. You did great." He leaned over his red basket, hamburger in one hand, napkin in the other. "Don't you want to go to college?"

I looked down at the ashtray, then across to the bar where Sylvia sat reading.

"I don't know." I looked at him. "I don't know."

"Well." Daniel shrugged, twitching his shoulders as he ate the rest of his hamburger and drank the last of his beer. He drinks funny. Instead of tilting the bottle and pouring beer into his mouth, he sucks at the top. When he pulls it away, the bottle pops from the suction.

"I don't." I lit another cigarette. This pack was half gone.

He slammed the empty bottle down and yanked a pen out of his back pocket. I could tell he was fired up; he kept clicking it in and out. "I can make some phone calls."

"Christ, Daniel."

Sylvia moved her mountain over to the table. "You done?" she asked, lifting one end of the basket with my hamburger and fries.

"Yeah," he answered.

She swept it and the rest up.

"Thank you," I said as she rolled back to the kitchen. Her big white polyester back looked like cottage cheese when the lid is first off. She never liked me much, even though I was quiet when I got drunk and left good tips. Never could understand her.

"How come you never showed me your poems, Daniel?" I lit another match just to watch it burn.

"Ames, come on."

15

"I'm serious."

"May we get back to the subject at hand?"

I blew out the little blue flame. "No."

He tapped his knuckles against the table top, out of rhythm with the clicking pen. "I get the sense you're not very interested in your education."

"That's not true. I'm very interested. But right now I'm more interested in your poems and how come I've never read them."

Staring at the frosted glass windows that faced Seventh Street, he clicked his pen slower and slower until he finally quit. "No artist is truly appreciated until after he is dead," he stated flatly, "particularly poets."

"Horse piss. Look at Lord Byron. Or Robert Frost. Or Rod McKuen."

"Rod McKuen isn't an artist, he's a jerk. So is Frost. And Byron is the exception, not the rule." He moved his head enough to see me. "Byron lived in a time when poetry was studied for its complexities, not printed on Hallmark cards." He flattened out another napkin and started writing.

I blew a smoke ring. "I'll drink to that," I said. I was starting to get a little buzzed with only a pop tart between me and the beer. Daniel just kept scribbling away like he was all by himself and not paying me any attention.

"So, boss," I drawled, sounding like I came right out of the hills without shoes or a shower to my name, "how come you never made a move on me?"

He looked up from his napkin, chin stuck on his chest and mouth hanging so far open I could count cavities. "What?"

I raised an eyebrow, something I'd been practicing for weeks. "Read my lips. How come you never made a move on me?"

"Cut it out, Ames," he said, blushing a little tiny bit, almost enough to be taken for a sunburn, except it wasn't there a minute ago. "Do you really want to see my poetry?"

"Uh huh. But only if we can fuck afterwards."

That tore him. For a worldly guy, he sure got embarrassed easy.

"Amory, come on." He looked around the room like it was full of people dying to overhear us. "Why are you doing this?"

"You're kind of cute when you blush."

"I don't blush," he said, now looking like he was running a low fever, "so stop it, Ames, I don't like being teased."

"I'm not teasing."

He drank some beer. Pop, the bottle went.

"Ever cut your lips doing that?"

"Doing what?"

"Nothing." I blew another smoke ring that he waved away. "When can I read your poems?"

"Tomorrow. I'll bring them to the shop."

"Great," I said, picking up my bottle, "great."

* * * * *

The phone rang over and over. I stumbled out to the kitchen, my hair feeling starched straight up, and my skin fuzzy like if someone poked me with a pin I'd say ouch some time next week.

"Hello?" I said, trying to rub the imprint of the couch off my face.

"Amy?"

17

I hate it when people call me Amy. "Yeah, this is me."
I yawned, barely able to get a cigarette out of the pack on
the table.

"This is Kendra Sites calling."

I tossed the pack. It skidded all the way to the other
end and fell over. "Hi."

"It seems the people who looked at your house
yesterday were very pleased with what they found."

I'd come home to find the closet door open and my shit
spilt all over the floor. "Yes?" Cigarette in my mouth, I
leaned over the stove and turned on the gas burner.

"They were pleased enough to make what I consider a
very reasonable offer."

"Damn!" I'd gotten too close to the flame and singed
my nose hairs.

"I'm sorry, I thought you would be pleased."

"I am, I am. So when do they want to move in?" Jesus,
that hurt. Felt like I was breathing fire.

"I'll let you know. I think they want to be in as soon
as possible. They've been looking for a new home in the
area for quite some time. Mr. Patterson is a new engineer
at Macon Mines —"

"Call me when you got a date."

"Well. All right."

"Thanks."

"You're welcome. Goodbye."

"Good —" Damn, she did it again.

I hung up and stretched, scratching under my shirt
where the scar itched. Suddenly hungry, I opened the
refrigerator to see if there was anything worthwhile to eat
and realized how long I'd been alone. It reeked like
something had crawled in between the lettuce and the
eggs and died. Christ. I slammed the door shut.

I took a shower and combed the wet mess of my hair on the drive to the shop. The book racks were out by the time I got there.

"Hey?"

"Hey," Daniel yelled back, "get over here and help me with this."

The bookstore was built like a bowling alley, all length and no width. Daniel was in the Romance Section, the suburbs of literature he called it, shoving books onto shelves without bothering to keep them alphabetical.

I walked back, every two steps giving a high wooden shelf a rap with my hand. I knew they were exactly four feet apart because I moved them last February when we had to make room for the three sofas. Daniel thought more people would come in if they had a place to sit down. I told him he was fucking nuts. People around here don't read anything but the address given for the special offers during soap operas and wrestling matches. They don't stop in very often, even though it's all cheap. Every month Daniel gets a U-Haul and takes off for a few days to hit garage sales and stores going out of business, coming back with his car, the Ghetto Jet, crammed full with boxes and stupid shit. That's how we got Rudolph. Daniel came back talking about how he'd gotten an antique for nothing and whipped out this foot-high ceramic bulldog. Rudolph was worth a mint till I turned him over and found the Made in Zanesville, Ohio, 1979, stamp on the bottom of his right foot. Now Rudolph sits on the desk with a copy of *The Sensuous Woman* balanced on his head.

The last book put away, double-checking to make sure the titles were all going in the same direction, I turned to Daniel. He was going through his list. He always carries a little scrap of paper in his back pocket with a list of all the stuff he's going to do that he's always revising. I've never seen him get everything done and throw the damn thing away.

"Daniel?" I leaned against the Philosophy Section shelf.

"Uh huh?" He added something to the list, trying to write with the paper cupped in his palm.

I handed him a book to write on.

"Thanks," he said, taking it and scribbling some more.

"Did you bring your poems?"

"What was that?" His eyebrows went up though his eyes didn't.

"Your poetry. You said I could read it. Did you bring any?"

"I sure did." He folded the paper neatly along the creases and tucked it and the pen away. "Just like I said I would."

I took the book back. *Philosophy of Human Travel*, Mivelman, was stamped in gold along the spine. "Can I see them?"

"When will you be free?"

"When will I be free? What kind of weird shit is that, when will I be free?" I snorted. He knew exactly what I did every day. I put the book back on the shelf between Mintner and Mizurski.

"I meant, when can we both sit down and read and discuss it together."

"Together?"

"I'm going to read it to you. That's the only way to really get the feel of the work." He said each word chopped like someone trying to sound British on TV.

Dropping his hands to his hips, he stepped closer. "How about now?"

"Well, see, I was going to ask you about that. Somebody's buying the house and I'm not done packing all of me and Jessie's shit. Think I could take the day off?"

"Could you wait till I finish with some things? Till noon or so?"

"Sure."

"Think you'll finish with the house by this evening?"

"Should."

"Then you could come over to my apartment and we could talk." One arm was draped across his waist, his hand propping up his elbow, and he was scratching under his chin the way someone would pet a cat.

I looked him square back, feeling like he was daring me to say yes. "Sure."

"Maybe we can get something to eat afterwards."

Nodding, I walked past him. I don't like it when people stare, and I almost turned around to say something trashy to make him stop but changed my mind.

The window nearest the door couldn't stay open by itself since its hinge hung like a dead spider leg, so I propped it open with Rudolph. It was a wasted effort against the heat but it gave me something to do for two minutes.

Grabbing a book off the desk, I flopped onto the middle sofa. It was brown and tan and black plaid, just long enough for me to stretch out my legs without letting anybody else sit down.

"That any good?" Sarcasm cooled the still air.

I turned to page seventeen. "No."

"Then why are you reading it?"

"Because it's too hot to read anything worth thinking about."

"Why that book? It certainly looks deep."

"I like the cover." It was of an Arab leaning down from a rearing horse to catch a blonde lady fainting in the desert. I felt his hand on my ankle.

"Move your legs, will you?"

"But I just hit the intellectual part."

"Amory."

I swung around to give him room.

Daniel sat down on the edge of the sofa where the wood stuck out from under the cushion. "Let's talk."

I plopped the book face down on the floor. "Okay, boss."

"Ames, I don't think you're going to be here much longer."

That was a shocker. "What?"

"Relax, relax, I'm not going to fire you or anything. But —" He bit his lip, "about school —"

"Jesus H. Christ on a go-cart, Daniel." I turned away. Daniel keeps the lights off on the hot days, so the edges of the bookshelves faded to gray with the gold and silver stamping of the important books sparking against the back wall.

"Okay, I know you think it's none of my business but I'm concerned you're not giving it enough thought."

I swung back to him. "I told you I would, Daniel, and I am."

The hot white light of the day came off the sidewalk and glared into the door and the windows behind him, turning his face a shadow. "I don't want to make you angry. I want to be sure you're thinking about your future." He stared at the ground. "And of our future."

Our future. "This is too much," I said, standing up. "I'm going home now, okay?"

"Okay. I think that may be a good idea." He tried to smooth out a wrinkle in the fake oriental rug with the toe of his tennis shoe. "I'll see you later?" he asked, eyes huge in his face when he looked up at me.

As I touched his shoulder his hand came up to catch mine. I walked away, holding on till our fingers brushed.

"Yes," I answered from the door.

* * * * *

The nightmare'd come.

I woke up, the house dark from the storm and smelling like lightning and my heart still pounding loud enough to hear it. I lit a cigarette. Fuck, it's the same, always the same, maybe I am going crazy, maybe Bobby was right. He'd look at me sort of sideways and say all the time, you're losing it, Amy, honey, you are going looney tunes.

But it's only a dream, a fucking dream.

The cigarette burned halfway and hissed. The ember was steaming away the ring of sweat my fingers left.

I can't stand it, I wish someone was here.

Numbers glowed a digital neon green from my clock radio. 6:42. I'd slept for five hours. Pulling my knees up, I wrapped the rest of myself around them and listened for creepy sounds, but heard only the rain fall, hardly loud in the quiet of the house. The air was thick and heavy. The rain hadn't washed the heat away, just chased it to the second floor where it was caught like a cat in flypaper. Buttoning my cut-offs, I walked down the dark hall past Jessie's room, where the only light was turning everything the color of bad weather.

23

I got in the car and drove across town to Daniel's. The water that the storm sent skating across the windshield sank into the hot tar, turning to a white mist that billowed like grounded clouds. A slow yawning aloneness crept up my legs promising to move further and I got to feeling like I was the only human being left, as if the world had ended and they forgot to tell me. Then I was caught at a railroad stop all red lights and clanging alarms and saw three guys in dirty overalls and baseball caps hanging out the caboose.

* * * * *

Daniel swung the door open and stepped back. "Come on in," he said. "Did you get your packing finished?"

"Not all of it. I fell asleep," I answered as the door swung shut behind me.

"I made iced tea. Would you like some?" he asked, quiet as the mist.

I shrugged. "Sure."

He stood there pulling on his moustache. "I'll be back in a second," he said, walking to the kitchen.

I looked for a place to sit down.

"You can move some of the stuff if you want," he called out, reading my mind.

I stacked up the books on the couch and searched for an unused place on the floor to put them.

"Here you go," he said. I set the last pile of paperbacks under what was once a living plant and took the glass he was holding out. We made to sit down.

"Shit, grab this," he half-shouted while sinking into the cushions.

24

The iced tea was safe. Daniel was stuck in the couch. I tried not to laugh. Didn't try hard enough and pretty soon we were both laughing to beat the band.

"I ought to get rid of this couch. A whole bunch of the springs are somewhere up in Connecticut." He stuck out his hand. I put the iced tea on the floor and helped him out. He flopped further over, so when I sat down I was practically in his lap.

He sipped his tea. He'd put too much sugar in mine. I put my glass on the furthest stack of books I could reach and pretended it wasn't there.

"When did it start raining?"

"Around four, four-thirty," he answered. "Storm blew up all of a sudden." He stared around me to look out the windows. "God, I love the rain. Maybe I'll go to Seattle after all."

"You ever been to Seattle?"

"No, but I think I'd like it. It rains a lot, a slow, heavy rain, and everything is green and rich."

"If you've never been there then how do you know?"

"Because a friend told me, that's how."

"I hate rain. The sky gets gray and streaky like dirty snow."

"That's air pollution from the mines damaging everything, even the clouds. If you were somewhere else you would probably love the rain as much as I do."

"No, I wouldn't. It makes me feel like I'm getting the chink water torture."

"That's Chinese, Amory. Walls have chinks."

"And they get plastered, just like Mr. Wozniak."

"Who's he?"

"The high school principal."

25

"How do you know he gets plastered?"

"Hell, Daniel, everybody knows that."

Daniel slurped. "Why don't you like the rain, really?" he said over the glass.

"Because I don't like getting spit on. Getting caught in a storm is like being in the middle of a football field with everybody in the stands chewing tobacco and taking aim."

"But it washes everything clean. Walking in the rain makes me feel brand new."

"That's good for you, Daniel," I mumbled. A strange pinching in my stomach started, as if I was going to puke right then and there. I tightened my jaws and crossed my arms, but it faded as quick as it came.

"You'd like the rain if you were somewhere else, I'm sure of it. Maybe you could go to Oregon or Washington, there are some good universities out there."

"There you go, ready to ship me out."

"I don't want to cause trouble, Ames, but you have to make a decision. I just want it to be the right one."

"Hell, Daniel, don't be asking me to think that far ahead." I stared down at my feet, watching my toes through the holes of my high top tennis shoes and feeling like one of those bag ladies they show on TV.

"Amory, what's wrong?"

I shrugged and looked out the window. This all seemed too strange. I stood up, trying to untie the straggles in my hair and shake this feeling of being so tiny.

"Come on back and sit down, babe. What's going on?"

"It's that fucking house. It's fucking haunted."

He patted the place next to him where I'd been sitting three seconds ago. I sat down, leaning on my elbows over my knees.

"You're selling the house, right?"

26

I nodded.

"Then what's the problem?"

"I can't stand living alone anymore," I said, looking at him.

Daniel set his glass on the floor and leaned back against the couch.

I sat up straight and took a deep breath. "Can I live here with you, Daniel, please?" My stomach tightened to a pinch again.

"What?"

"Just till I go to school? Can I? May I?"

It was his turn to run his hand through his hair and not look at me. I put my hand on his arm and his fingers knitted and unknitted.

"Please, Daniel?" The pinch tightened then let go, gushing down my legs and up my back at the same time to push goosebumps to the top of my skin.

He pulled at a few hairs on the left side of his lip. "Why with me?"

My knees bobbed up and down. "Because you're my best friend, I don't have anywhere else to go, weird shit goes on in that house and I'll pay rent."

He smiled his usual close-lipped smile, fingers resting on his bottom lip. His eyes got thinner while he tilted his chin up, like his face was on automatic pilot as he scanned me. "Why are you so nervous?"

"Because you're looking at me strange."

He finally looked away to the windows, then to the stacks of books on the floor. "I guess I am," he murmured, facing me again. "I'm sorry."

A car went by, loud because it didn't have a muffler. I craned my neck, trying to see who it was. Daniel caught my hands, his fingers damp from the sides of the glass where rivulets of cold sweated down the slick amber. I turned back.

"I didn't mean to make you uncomfortable. I just like the way you look," he said, staring at my mouth.

He hardly kissed me, just a peck. I loosened my hands, slid them up to his face to hold him steady then laid one on him. Daniel kissed back. His mouth tasted like iced tea and sugar and peppermint toothpaste, and he was much better at this than Bobby. Bobby would stick his tongue in my mouth and leave it there like an old worm or something while he unzipped his jeans.

"I haven't made out on a couch since I was fifteen." He finally spoke when we came up for air.

I brushed his hair back. "How old are you, anyway?"

"I should be asking you that."

"You know I'm nineteen. What if you're jailbait?"

He smiled. "I'm twenty-six." He pulled at my hair like he was trying to make some of the curls go straight. "You're surprised?"

"A little."

"How old did you think I was?"

I looked him square in the eye. "Twelve."

"No, really."

"I never gived it much thought." That was a lie. I thought he was closer to Bobby Lee's age, twenty-three.

"You never gave, Ames. Gived is not a verb."

"You knew what I meant, didn't you?"

He grinned and hugged me to him. "Yes, I knew what you meant." He felt good and smelled like soap and pretty soon we were giggling like little kids who buried the gym whistle in the school sandbox. I pulled away to look at him.

He held my face. "When can you move in?"

"When do you want me?"

"I want you now Amory," he answered, serious again, the laughing gone.

"I'll move in tomorrow then," I said, leaning over to kiss him.

* * * * *

His hand was warm as he led me to his bedroom in the back. The windows framed the clouds that broke enough to let the sunset slip through, and the light poured in over the sills. The sky was a sidewalk gray cracked with a stream of orange and magenta thick enough to take a bite.

Clothes fell light to the floor and we dropped to his bed, rolling and hungry, mouths seeming fused together. I locked my legs around his hips and he slid inside, freezing still as the last second of sun gleamed over him like a halo. Both of us were slick with sweat and friction. By the time he got done, the sun was gone and I could barely see him in the nighttime heat. Gently I twisted away and he rolled on his back.

I slid my hands over him. His skin was smooth compared to Bobby's, and his hips were narrower. I rubbed his arms, his chest, brushed the coarse hairs of his belly and his thighs. Daniel might have been a long distance runner once, maybe even real good, but not now. There was too much looseness in his waist, not like the beer gut Bob had, but like he was letting himself slip away. I curled next to him, tracing the slats of his ribs. He was breathing quieter now, chest moving slow beneath my fingers. Deep disappointment seeped through my hands and clung to my bones. So this is it. Like a Christmas present wrapped up so pretty that the gift inside is nothing like what the outside promises.

Daniel moved his head, trying to see my belly in the dark. "So that's the other scar?"

I nodded, my cheek moving against his shoulder with a round, moist sound.

"Jesus, I'm, uh, sorry." He rolled to his side. "That wasn't what I wanted to say. I suppose you don't want to talk about it?"

There was no point in answering. My eyes got used to the light bouncing off the white ceiling and walls. He was curled as I was, his arm my pillow and our knees touching, two shapes white and ghost-like. I could stay here, we could live in Sterling. I kissed his mouth, a red flash behind my eyes mixing with shades of gray. I might even fall in love with him. He kissed back as if he meant it.

"I really am sorry," he said again as he gently pushed me onto my back.

* * * * *

I kissed Daniel's back and when he turned over kissed him good morning and goodbye. Taking his key, I stepped into the day, hoping T & D's Hardware would be open. Coming back, I heard the shower running. I left a note and his key ring. I had to finish with the house.

There was only my shit and Jessie's room to be cleared out since I'd gotten the other rooms finished yesterday. Jessie didn't have much — clothes, prayer books, stuff like that. I started with her closet and threw everything into boxes: her six pairs of sensible shoes, dresses hung by color from light to dark, belts and scarves hung on the inside hooks and full of dust because she hardly ever wore them but liked the bright colors. She didn't wear pants either, said it wasn't right for a woman who worked for the church, said that people who might otherwise learn

30

about Jesus might miss the opportunity because they thought a woman in pants too forward. Once I said if people really wanted religion they would listen to anybody who knew anything even if they were stark raving naked. Her face got her meanest shade of red, then a different yellow-gray I'd never seen before, the same color as the pages of books that have been sitting in somebody's attic for a million years and are starting to mold. When she went into the hospital she stayed that color, and when she tried to talk her mouth looked like she'd been chewing rubber cement. It was funny; up till then I always thought death was white and graceful, like a swan.

That was the first time we disagreed on something that she didn't take a swing at me. I thought it was because she thought maybe I really was right, but it was because she was sick and wouldn't tell anybody except maybe her god. She would never tell me anything even if I could help. I wasn't that bad as a kid, but I sure was no Shirley Temple on the Saturday Afternoon Matinee neither. Not that Jess didn't try. She once made me take tap lessons. Soon as she dropped me off at the Y, I'd kick off my shiny black dance shoes and jump in the pool wearing my little leotard thing. My hair would still be wet when she came to pick me up, but she must have thought I was working up quite a sweat learning how to shuffle off to Buffalo because she didn't say a thing. I managed to keep that up for a couple weeks till she noticed the purple leotard was fading to light blue from the chlorine and getting stretched to hell from me taking it off to swing around my head, whipping the water out to get it dry.

Making me take tap was her way of trying to turn me into a lady. That's why she wouldn't let me play with boys. For a long time my only friend was Annabelle Leisch who lived down the street on the other side of the Cornfelds. She had an Easy Bake Oven that could cook stuff with a light bulb. We'd make cakes, eat them when they were only half done and be sick the rest of the night. We weren't friends anymore by junior high, when she moved away. She got pregnant right after, had the kid and kept it.

I'm never going to have kids. I told Jessie once and she threw some of her religiousness at me, saying marriage and pregnancy were a woman's purpose. I said bullshit, no way am I going to stay home vacuuming the floors and depending on some jerk to make the money, I have better things to do with my time. Like what? she said, and I said like go to college, maybe learn how to be an architect or a writer. She started laughing crazy-mean, then she stopped laughing and got a grip on my hair and screamed at me to watch my mouth. I don't think she'd have gotten so upset if I hadn't asked why she didn't ever fulfill her woman's purpose.

Two boxes filled fast. Shoes, skirts, statues, it didn't matter if it got mixed up, the Goodwill people were getting all of it. When I'd take a picture off the wall, I'd frisbee it into the nearest box, giving it just enough spin to land flat without breaking the glass. There were lots of religious pictures, old rugged crosses and one ice cream social picture with me standing on the end, a big-eyed kid waving like an idiot and holding a paper plate full of ice cream and a hunk of Mrs. Homer's chocolate cake that Jess chopped for me to eat, even though I couldn't. She used to say I was so skinny people'd think I was a starved child so she was always feeding me to prove I wasn't mistreated.

I think maybe she did that stuff because she wasn't really my aunt. I showed up when she was working at Our

Lamb Baptist Church one day and she put on such a grand show of Christian charity she won the grand prize — me.

I'm standing off by myself in this picture because there were a lot of people at that social — Jessie had been head of the committee and wanted to raise more money than anybody ever had — and I wanted to be sure I could find myself. I was only ten years old at the time, but she didn't think it was very funny, said I was showing off. I remember that social really well not only because of all the people but because Jess and Mrs. MacElfresh, who'd been on the committee the year before and said Jessie's publicity was vulgar, got into a shouting fight right there on the lawn of Our Lamb Baptist. Mrs. MacElfresh showed up at the hospital the same day I called Daniel at his parents' house, when the doctors knew Jessie was going to die and I did, too, but nobody was saying anything. She tried to tell me to be strong, that Jesus Christ was standing beside me in this time of hardship. I told her god moved to Beverly Hills in 1956 and has been drinking piña coladas in the sun ever since.

A white box fell from the bottom of a drawer I had turned over into a carton. I'd been emptying the drawers that way since it was faster than shoveling the stuff out stack by stack. I pulled it out and opened it up. Inside was a blue felt scrapbook with Memories stamped in silver on the front. The pages were black and heavy, like construction paper, and the first page had Jessie Cassandra Walker written on a piece of white paper glued to the middle. I don't think she ever told me her middle name was Cassandra.

The next page held pictures, brown and white instead of black and white, of three girls. Special portraits for high school graduation because Mike Goff Photography was printed on the corner and Mike Goff Junior still does everything for the yearbook. Each girl's wearing a white blouse and I can tell the one in the middle is Jess. She's cute with her hair brushed back, her face round and giggly. She even has her eyebrows, instead of being plucked away and penciled on.

The girl on the right looks like a cheerleader, like Suzie Munson. Everyone was always saying how she was a beauty queen, and all the guys were killing themselves to get a date with her. But this girl's face is painted on, all fake, and her pageboy haircut with ends that point out is really stupid looking. Shit, does she look familiar. It isn't Kendra Sites. It isn't May Ellen Frotch who died in a car wreck when I was six.

I stuck a thumbnail under a corner and peeled the photo back, real careful because the old tape was tearing bits of the picture. Sylvia Ann Carter it says on the back. With all my love and friendship, Sylvia Ann Carter. I'll be damned. I flipped it back over. Sylvia. Jesus, has she changed. I smashed it down with the palm of my hand but it wasn't sticking very well. Me and Sylvia never did get along. What wiped off that expression that said the world was her cereal box and she just found the prize inside?

I didn't recognize the girl on the left, though I felt that I should have. She looks like the kind of person who'd wear nice perfume that stays in the air after she leaves. Her hair's wavy and light, not dark like the other two, and tied back with a ribbon. She's wearing a pearl necklace that falls perfect on her neck at the collarbones, and since she's looking into the camera, I can see her whole face, her strong high cheekbones making her eyes slant a little, and her mouth set as if she was about to smile full and clear. Wonder who she is? Cellophane tape stringing, I peeled the photo off the page. Faded blue was

34

smeared on the back and a fingerprint in the corner; someone had picked it up before the signature had time to dry. Joanna. Joanna somebody. Joanna with no last name, she was no one. Joanna Nobody. I wonder if she knows her face is in a dead woman's pile of memories.

From the next page on it's me all over. Me as a baby, me in first grade, me on a trike, even me in the bathtub. There were pictures the school took all the way up to sixth grade. That was the year Jessie got her Polaroid and she was always pulling it out, though she never did figure out how to put the film in right. And there's the picture of me and Skeeter, my dog, just before he got hit by a car. There's my singing group in junior high school, the shot she took when we went caroling and walked all the way out here. I was fifteen and told her we'd be stopping by. She must not have heard me because when she opened the door that night to find out what all the racket was, she was wearing her oldest bathrobe. First she got embarrassed, then she got excited and ran to get her camera instead of staying on the porch to listen to us. She came back out and had to walk through the drifts to get a good angle, she said. There I'm in the front row, trying to look holy while singing "Silent Night" to Jessie in the snow.

The pictures stopped after that. I thumbed the last empty pages, thinking maybe I skipped something, but no. No clippings from track and field, nothing. I closed the book. There couldn't be any more pictures after that spring anyway since she gave away her camera to the church charity auction and I didn't have Mike Junior take my senior picture.

It'd gotten so strange between us. Maybe because me and Bobby were spending so much time together after I got out of the hospital. She hated him, she even said so, hated me going out with him, especially when I didn't come home nights, but she never threw me out, hardly ever said a thing but that I'd regret my evil in the end.

I opened the cedar chest at the foot of her bed, shoving the quilt off only to feel guilty enough to re-fold it and put it in a box. Inside were lacy tablecloths and napkins, the real stuff; I could tell because they felt thick and dainty at the same time, and were wrapped in plastic to stop them from yellowing. It was Jessie's hope chest, what she'd been saving in here for years and years, the last years without any hope at all. It got too weird. Here was this woman by turns pushing her religion on me, then not caring what I did. It wasn't like Jess decided she would leave me in peace. She'd butt in all the time to tell me what to do or she'd start yelling for no reason. She would look at me funny, especially if she'd been to the china hutch one too many times, and say, Amory, life ain't a three-ring circus for you to be clapping at all the time. It was the only time she'd say ain't, and she got to saying it over and over, like she was trying to tattoo my eardrum.

I closed the cedar chest and put the book on the bureau so's not to forget it. It was going back to Daniel's with me. Jess never liked Daniel. She was never rude to him, but she didn't like him just the same. He's different and he'd say right out loud that I should go to college and that bugged her. She didn't think I could make it in a million years. I don't think I'd ever let my kid know I thought something like that. I'd lock it away in the back of my brain so far back I'd learn how to forget it.

Everything from Jessie Cassandra Walker's life was finally packed into six boxes and left at Goodwill.

Back at the house, I left the car radio cranked up so high I could hear it in my bedroom. Shoving, kicking, and swearing, I managed to get all my junk into the Buick. Then I headed across town. For a split second as I stepped into the apartment, I thought Daniel was waiting for me in his bedroom. I stacked my boxes by the door and got my stuff upstairs without too much of a hassle. The trunk was a bitch to haul, but I got that in, too.

Dropping my shirt in the hallway, I walked toward the bathroom. Daniel's apartment was small, almost too small for one person much less two. But I'll be gone soon. I turned on the bath water. The light from the kitchen windows hit the tile in there and reflected in the mirror, throwing itself into twists and bends. I'll be gone from this town and from Jessie and from all the people who think they know more about me than I do. I'll get so far away they'll never touch me again or come knocking at my door. When the water was at halfway, I shucked off my shorts and got in, the cool water like light green ink.

* * * * *

I somehow got into Chase University, where Daniel had gone to college. It all happened with me watching like it was a TV show. The house and everything in it was sold, and by August I wrecked the Buick, paid my tuition and started smoking two and a half packs a day. Daniel and I slept together and sometimes we made love with the lights on but most of the time we didn't.

I shipped my boxes that had spent the summer by the door, packed up anything I had lying around and got on a plane that was to fly me two thousand miles away from Sterling, West Virginia. Daniel offered to drive me, but I said no, I wanted to go alone. I got on the plane and flew like dust and ghosts through the air.

Dooley Hall is a dorm with two wings. One side has the girls and one side has the guys and we're kept apart by a huge fucking staircase everybody calls the Twilight Zone. I have my own room and a stereo to keep me

37

company. It's not that I get lonely, really. I miss Daniel, especially at night when I roll over on my little single bed and practically fall out reaching for him, but I'm not homesick. It's more like a TV sitcom going at superfast speed and I'm getting motion sickness. The dream comes sometimes, though no one ever says anything about me making noise. Maybe they think I sneak a guy into my room every night and have such a good time I can't keep my mouth shut.

* * * * *

"Ames! Amory!"

I looked around the terminal, trying to see over the heads of all the people. I was still feeling claustrophobic from the accordion walkway out of the plane, so it wasn't easy to balance on my toes. The two glasses of wine didn't help either. I finally saw Daniel, waving like a crazy man. Good thing I found him; I was getting charley horses in my feet.

"Amory, baby." He hugged tight enough to practically knock the wind out of me. It was good to see him, but I wished he'd let me set my bookbag down. It was the only thing I'd brought from college and I was sure going to try to forget it was mine. Forget it, forget the teachers, forget the girls and the boys trying to be so cool and so smart. They weren't any smarter than me; I got in, too.

Driving into town was long and cold in the Ghetto Jet. Daniel kept asking questions that I answered a long time ago. Is David Herron still chairman of the English Department? Who got thrown into the pond after the first snow? Does Bess the cleaning lady still sing gospel over the roar of the vacuum cleaner?

38

"You know, Ames," he said, finally disgusted, "I am really making an effort to talk with you and you're not helping in the least."

"I'm tired and there isn't much to say except please turn up the heat. You know what Chase is like. You went there for six years." I bunched further into my peacoat, the wool feeling scratchy and warm on the sides of my face.

"But I want to know if it's any different."

"I wasn't there when you were so I can't tell you."

He was quiet a moment, letting that sink in. "Is it the way I said it would be?"

The muscles in my sides were starting to ache from trying to stay warm. "I don't know, I guess so," I lied. It was nothing like he said it would be. Nobody talked about anything, nobody looked at anything. Just sat around picking their noses all the time.

"Like how?"

"Shit, Daniel, do we have to talk about this on the first day of my Christmas vacation?"

"I'm sorry," he said, pulling me over and kissing my forehead, his eyes still on the freeway, "I haven't been very considerate."

The rest of the ride was quiet except for KGDB coming over the airwaves for all of northern West Virginia. Daniel drove and I played with a single white feather that had escaped from his blue down jacket. I'd hold it up a bit and let it fall, watching it drift to my lap. It was made perfect for flying, made for wrapping around an animal and helping it get into the air.

"Are you hungry?" he asked after thirty miles of commercial free pop rock.

"Yep." I stretched the feather, uncurling it. There were close to fifty wisps all ordered according to length and width. Somehow it made sense that a bird could fly using these little pieces of nothing.

"Would you like to stop somewhere?"

"Jake's." I let the feather float from my fingers.

Sylvia was coming off her shift and we had to back out of the doorway to let her through. She didn't say a thing, not an excuse me or anything, but I had the old picture of her hid in Jessie's scrapbook to laugh over, and forgave Sylvia her bad manners. Me and Daniel had the place to ourselves and sat in our booth. He got up to put a few quarters in the jukebox and pretty soon the place filled with the old tunes, just loud enough to be heard over the electric noise of the video games against the wall.

Straight-armed with her ass almost knocking the chairs over, a waitress ambled over, moving like somebody greased her hips but forgot her elbows bend, too. Jess'd say a girl like that was nothing but trash, but at least she walked like a woman. She used to say I strut like a poor man who just won the lottery.

* * * * *

"So where's my Christmas present?" I asked as we lay in bed, blankets shoulder high.

"Jews don't believe in Christmas."

"Should've told me before I bought the Porsche."

He half-laughed and sat up to turn on the reading lamp that stretched over the bed. Handing the ashtray to me, he took two cigarettes out of my pack, lit them both and handed me one. He pulled the blanket further up his chest then took the ashtray away, setting it on his thigh. "So you want your Christmas present?"

"Uh huh. It better be a good one. I dropped a bundle on you this year."

40

"Oh, it is."

"Where is it?"

"You're looking at it."

"Gee, what a surprise."

Daniel tried to blow a smoke ring. "I'm going back to Chase with you."

Shit. "What?"

"I missed you, babe. I want to be with you. I want to get my degree. I want us to be some place where people won't freak out about us sleeping together."

"They don't do that here."

"Yes, they do." His voice went flat. "They're always thinking about how that Jew's screwing Jessie Walker's girl."

"Bullshit." I flicked my cigarette. "Fuck them if they can't take a joke."

"It's not a joke. It's true, Amory. I know it is."

"Did somebody tell you that to your face?"

"I know all about anti-Semitism, Ames. I can sense it."

"I'm sure you can." I sat up.

"What's that supposed to mean?"

"Nothing, nothing. Go on."

"But there's something more important at stake." He looked from the wall and at me. "I want us to talk. I hate telephones, so I never talk to you. And for a writer, you're terrible about letters."

I'd been a shit about that. Nothing ever seemed important enough to write down.

"Besides," he went on, "I think I'm ready to get some work done."

I crushed out my half-smoked cigarette. Funny how things stop tasting good after having them. "What do you mean?"

"I came to Sterling to be around the people here, the people who work with their hands. I wanted to write about them, put their lives, their visions in my poetry. I've been all over the world and I thought the people here were real. Everyone is so poor, they have a certain wealth, a certain pride, a certain —" His hand fluttered outward, smoke trailing behind, "simplicity."

The word echoed in my head, the sound of it stretching down my throat and tying around my voice. "What did you say?" I whispered.

"Simplicity. I thought I'd find it here." He dragged on the cigarette. "But it's all changed for me, Amory." He put his hand on his bare chest, fingers balancing his palm like a five-legged table. "I need a new environment. I'm suffocating."

"Suffocating?" Simplicity. The thin razor-edged curl of the word cut through his sentences, slicing neat lines.

"Suffocating. No, drowning, drowning in the racism, the conservatism, all of it." His fingers bounced off his chest with each word. "I can't write here."

Simplicity. He said it so easy, like it didn't really mean anything. Simplicity.

"A poet must be in a place that allows him to expand his language. I don't feel safe enough here."

"Hell." I sighed. His shoulders were hunched forward, his body intent on making me understand. Simplicity. I rubbed my eyes. "Go to Paris then."

"I don't have the money."

"How are you going to pay for school?"

"My parents will help with that." He shrugged and inhaled on the cigarette. It stuck from between his fingers, looking strange because he cupped his hand while he smoked as if to hide his mouth. "That's how I kept the bookstore open."

I slid back down under the covers.

"If you don't want me, just say so."

I took his cigarette, the ash falling into the sheets, and put it out. "Of course I want you," I said, "you know I do. I miss making love with you, miss the times when you roll over and ask me to make you coffee even though it's two o'clock in the morning."

He rolled over on top of me and I kissed him on the lips.

"I miss you, too, babe. You're so far away from me. All I can think about is how much I love you."

* * * * *

I'm here, right here. It's only a dream.

Over and over, like a prayer I say it, lying trapped in oily sweat next to Daniel.

I can still smell the new grass growing between snow-crushed weeds under me. Seeing his face, feeling red pain scatter like leaves in the wind, memories like steel traps biting deep and all I can do is run. Run in the forest, like running underwater, trying to go faster because he's right behind me, smelling the blood and getting stronger with the scent. The silent breaking of my body through the trees, running as if on black ice, though I didn't run away from him that day in the afternoon sun. Didn't scream, didn't tear away as he babbled crazy things I couldn't understand. Simplicity, he'd said, want simplicity.

Daniel slept on beside me, a flat white thing as I waited for the pounding that about pushed veins through my skull to slow down. Wake up, Daniel, I almost said, trying to send a message into his dream, wake up and cradle me with your body. But he was quiet and still. I felt

43

strange now in this bed next to him, my man who'd touched me and made love to me. I slipped my arms around his waist and lay my cheek between his shoulder blades.

He jerked suddenly, half-turning to his side.

"I'm sorry, Daniel, I'm sorry, I didn't mean to wake you up."

"I can't lay like that." His voice was thick with sleep. "I move around too much."

I rolled onto my back, thinking and waiting and watching Christmas morning go from black to gray to white through the windows of the room.

* * * * *

I gave Daniel his presents at breakfast. He liked the sweater and loved the running shoes. By lunchtime I was bored.

"I'm going out," I said as he sat at the kitchen table poring over stray sheets of paper.

"Where?"

I grabbed my peacoat and scarf. "Just out."

"Do you need the car?"

"Naw. I can walk." I slammed the door behind me. Damn, I forgot my gloves on the counter near the clock. I pulled out a cigarette and took three matches to get it lit. Daniel asked me once why I didn't buy a lighter. I told him I didn't like them. I had one once, but it made me look like a hardcore smoker and I swore I'd quit as soon as I used that lighter up. It got lost right after that. He asked me why I didn't quit then. I told him to shut up.

Wind devils spun snow on the banks where it lay loose, lifting it up in a white sand dance. When I was little we used to chase the mini-tornadoes in autumn on the playground at school, trying to jump into the circling leaves.

I lit each cigarette from the end of the other as I walked across town. Sterling is always quietest on Easter Sunday and loudest on high school graduation night. Christmas, people are busy doing stupid things like shoveling the driveway. It's as if everybody in town is trying to get away from the people they're supposed to be overjoyed to see, like their kids.

Mine were the only footprints on this side of the hill, and there was no wind down here. Jessie's headstone was buried with new and old snow from this winter. I didn't brush or kick it away, figuring it sure as hell wasn't bothering her and it looked a lot better than the plastic flowers one grave over. I could read everything on her marker except the dates on the bottom. Last time I'd been here I couldn't see them either because the dirt was piled up around the sides of the hole and the sky was ready to break with the weight of rain and thunder. The ride had seemed so long as I sat in the back of that big black car though the funeral home was on the south side of town too, barely past the iron spear fence of the graveyard. And Bobby, in the dog-shit color suit and the box-toed shoes he wore, showing up even though I'd asked him not to. He never knew when to do the right thing. The only thing he knew was the mines, been working there so long coal dust was settled into the lines of his hands, turning wrist to finger into a scattered black road map.

I lit another cigarette, emptying the pack. I crushed it, the cellophane squeaking in the cold air, got ready to toss it, then changed my mind and shoved it back in my pocket. The sun slipped out from the clouds and I squinted from the too-white snow and the smoke of the cigarette hanging out the corner of my mouth.

"I don't know why I've come, Jess," I said, then inhaled and blew a smoke ring into the Christmas afternoon. Once I saw a movie about people who died and came back to life. One guy went on and on about a golden rope that tied the spirit to a body. Once it's broken, that person is dead without a hope of getting back, period. I leaned on my left leg, right hand coming out of my coat pocket and resting on my hip, a silent fuck you to the cold. I'll bet Jessie's spirit brought along the garden shears to ease her departure along, just to get away from me. I followed the edge of white against gray beneath her name with my eyes. At least no dog has pissed on her headstone yet.

I finished the cigarette, dropped it into a footprint and walked away.

* * * * *

"I'll call you when I get in," I said as we waited for my turn to board.

"I should be packed tomorrow. You'll look for an apartment?"

I nodded. The voice on the loudspeaker called the last seats. Sounded like she had metal lungs.

"Good." Daniel flashed his smile. "I miss you already."

"It's only three days." Hugging him with one arm, I kissed him quick then headed for the plane.

* * * * *

Monday came and Daniel did, too. He brought a backpack, a suitcase, and one box of books. I hadn't even started looking for an apartment, much less found one,

46

but Daniel's friend Drake had. The afternoon was flat and cold when Daniel came to pick me up to look at it. The building was a few blocks from campus and its halls were narrow and smelled like carpet glue and burnt hamburger.

As soon as the door closed, Daniel grabbed for me.

"Let me look around, for Christ's sake," I snapped. I didn't mean to sound so bitchy, but the weather was bad and he was being a pain in the butt.

I dropped my coat, soon covered by his jacket, and started wandering around. It was almost the same as his old apartment except there was red thread instead of blue in the gray carpet, different handles on the kitchen cupboards and the bathroom was yellow instead of green.

"You don't like it." He stood there kicking his toe against the floor. It didn't mater if I liked it or not; he'd already signed a six-month lease.

"It's fine," I said, pulling out a cigarette but not lighting it. "It'll be fine." I shoved the cigarette back in the pack, walked over and kissed him the way he'd been wanting me to since we got here. He put his forehead on mine, with one arm around my waist, and began undoing the buttons of my flannel shirt with one hand.

"What are you doing, Daniel?"

"I think it's time we checked out the bedroom."

"I already have."

"I think we should do it together."

"Doesn't it bother you that we don't have a bed?" I asked as the button past halfway slid open.

"We'll just have to fake it, baby," he answered pulling my shirttails out of my jeans. "You know, we don't need that bedroom after all." He stopped messing with my buttons and pulled his sweater over his head, static electricity snapping. "I think," he began, finishing with my buttons, "that more than anything else —" He slid the shirt off my shoulders and down my arms, leaving me shivering in my T-shirt, "I would like —" He nuzzled into my neck, leaning against me, "to make love to you."

"Please don't," I said quietly. He kissed my mouth, then bit my neck.

"I want you, Ames, I want you right here." His hands rubbed across my back, a brief second of warmth.

I flattened my palm against his chest, pushing a little to let him know I meant it. "It's too cold, Daniel."

"I'll keep you warm," he answered, dragging me to the floor and starting to knead my boobs as if they were bread dough. "I love you, Amory," he said, tugging at my zipper, "I want you so much, come on, baby, relax."

He pulled up my right leg then the left, untying my laces and shoving my boots half off. I grabbed my peacoat and threw it over us, still cold though he was on top of me.

"Don't worry about being warm," he whispered, his mouth bending the curve of my ear, "pretty soon you'll be hot enough for both of us."

He kept biting, his teeth sharp and hard at my skin. He tugged at my clothes, hands running over me like he was trying to find the right combination of buttons to push. I shoved at his shoulders. "When I say no, dammit, I mean it."

He leaned onto his haunches and looked down at me, my legs trapped beneath his.

"I know what will change your mind." He smiled, tight-lipped and his eyes half shut. He unzipped his jeans and pushed them down just low enough. The tip of his hard-on was eggplant-colored.

I sat up.

"What the hell is wrong?" he asked, his turn to be angry though I wasn't done yet.

"I'm cold," I said through gritted teeth.

"You're cold."

I reached for my shirt and pulled it on.

"You've never been cold before."

"There's no heat." I started buttoning the buttons and straightening out the rest of me.

"No heat. You didn't say that in the back seat of the car before you got on the plane."

"Stop it, Daniel."

"You stop it." He stood up, zipping his pants. "What's the matter with you? Ever since you left, it's like our relationship doesn't exist. Not writing to me. Not calling. Not even wanting to come back for the holidays. You know what's really cold? You are. You're like a fucking icicle."

Like fucking an icicle. I sighed and stared at the floor. I think I hate this carpet. "Let it go, Daniel."

"Fine," he said, grabbing his sweater, "that's just fine."

* * * * *

I borrowed a car that week and drove to the Salvation Army. By the time Daniel got back to the apartment, we had a queen size mattress and box spring that sank in the middle.

"You could buy some decent furniture, Amory."

"You could've kept yours instead of selling it. I'm not buying till I'm sure I can pay for it."

"Of all the things to worry about," he said, rolling his eyes, something he'd been doing more and more since he got here. "You have plenty of money. And you said you were looking for a job. This place could look great if you'd do something about it."

It wasn't worth fighting over, though we did. I kept looking for bargains and a job. I finally broke down and dropped a bundle on a brass bed frame and two desks. The bed squeaked, keeping me awake for a week, but the desks were great. One was five feet long and almost didn't get in the door. The other was a roll top, hand-made. Daniel sort of spread his shit on both of them; I didn't have enough room for my stamps.

* * * * *

Marielle had a laugh that sounded like she was gargling and by the end of my first week at the bookstore, she hated my guts. By the time classes started, though, she was too busy annoying everybody else to even bother with me.

"Unless these are filled out correctly, Professor Dawson," Marielle said, "I can't order the books for you." She gave the professor a wimpy look that was to pass for a smile. I guess she couldn't get anything else across her face, being so skinny. Jessie would've said it was a miracle she could make a shadow, she was so thin.

"I filled them out four months ago."

"And they were wrong then and they're wrong now," Marielle answered.

I kept re-stocking the bookshelves. The lady teacher kept calm, calmer than a lot of other people dealing with Marielle from what I'd seen in only one week of work. "What seems to be the problem?"

"They are lacking a signature of the instructor and the department chairman."

"My signature —"

"Is not enough to place an order with me. The Women's Studies Department hasn't gone through the Academic Advisory Council yet."

"But it will."

"I'm sorry, that's not good enough," Marielle sniffed. Picking up her inventory sheets, she pretended to scan titles all the way down the aisle till she stepped into the back.

Professor Dawson gritted her teeth. For a second I thought she was going to knock all the shelves over like giant dominoes. Wouldn't've bothered me, especially if Marielle got squashed flat as a bug underneath one. "Shit goddamn motherfucker," she muttered.

I must've looked pretty stunned when she noticed me staring.

"Sorry. Holdover vocabulary from my hippie days," she explained, not sounding sorry at all. "Do I have to order my text books through her?"

I nodded.

The professor slapped the shelf, hard enough to rock the souvenir coffee cups, swung around and stomped into the back room, looking like she was ready to eat bricks. She slammed the back room door shut, trapped inside with Marielle McCloskey.

By morning her books were ordered. I saw the invoice.

* * * * *

Three hours fucking around with my fall schedule, only to get stuck with either a women's studies class or ancient history. Ancient history, Christ, who needs it? I have enough trouble living in the present tense. Women's

Studies. At least that Dawson lady is teaching it. I sat on the steps of the Admin Building and lit a cigarette, watching the people skitter by on all sorts of business they thought important. The wind sifted through the new green leaves in the tops of the oak and dutch elm trees, turning them upside down and back again. Maybe Daniel can get me into Herron's Elizabethan Lit seminar.

It was chilly for May and I was glad I wore a sweatshirt. It said Eat Shit and Die on the front and was twelve sizes too big. I got it from Bobby Lee two years ago for my birthday and he said it fit perfect.

A girl walked by slower and slower till she stopped. She had incredible hair, auburn with gold glints that sparked with sunshine. The stripes of her rugby shirt reflected off her kelly green eyes as she watched me. I blew a smoke ring in her direction and she stood there till the circle broke up in the wind.

"Do you have a light?" she asked, walking over.

I dug into my pocket for matches.

"Thanks," she said, taking them from my hand. "Now, can I bum a cigarette?"

She sat down next to me, using two matches for the cigarette I'd pulled out of my pack for her.

"Thanks."

"Sure."

We sat and smoked for a little while.

"So tell me," the redhead began, "how it is that you can be as effortlessly beautiful as you are?"

* * * * *

I slammed the apartment door behind me. I always forget that it shuts automatically even though I've been locked out a couple of times taking out the trash and doing laundry. Who the fuck is she? At least I managed to mumble something before jumping up and practically running away. Daniel will know her, he knows everybody. I could hear him in the bedroom, pounding away at his typewriter.

"Daniel?" I rushed in, breathing too hard to talk right. Felt like I'd done the fifty yard dash to win the Presidential Award for Physical Fitness. "Daniel, hey, I got to talk to you."

"What?" he asked, still typing.

"Do you know, hey, would you listen to me for a second?"

He kept on. I stepped around his chair and unplugged the cord. He looked at me, pissed and not even trying to hide it.

"Now, would you listen to me?"

"What do you want?"

"Do you know a red-haired girl with green eyes?"

Daniel stood up and took the cord away from me. "Only about a hundred or so." He bent down and soon the typewriter was humming. "Does she know me?" he asked, sitting down again.

"I don't know. I didn't ask. She's my height, really good-looking, and her hair is red, redder than yours, though not as dark." I touched the top of his head. His hair was almost brown.

"Is she from around here?" he asked, typing as he spoke.

"I guess so. She sat on the steps of the Admin Building with me."

"Really?" He tilted his head as if he was listening to me but I knew he wasn't; the typewriter hadn't stopped clacking since he'd plugged it back in.

"She asked me how I could be so effortlessly beautiful," I said, biting my lip.

"Really?" This got his interest. He stopped typing. "And what did you say?"

"What did I say? What could I say? I left. Damn, I think she still has my matches."

"Was she thin, with a great set of tits?"

"I wasn't looking at her tits, Daniel," I snapped. Bastard.

"Women watch women more than men watch women, Amory, it's a statistical fact." The typewriter cracked as letters hit the paper again. "You could've at least said thank you. You can consider it quite a compliment."

"Why? Who was she?"

He typed a paragraph then stopped again. His teeth flashed in a cocky grin, bright white like a shark's. "That, my dear, was Cady, spelled C-A-D-Y, Baird. Superdyke."

I walked out of the room as the typewriter clapped.

A superdyke? That pretty girl is a lesbian? I guess it makes sense seeing what she said, but she sure didn't look like one. She wasn't decked out in lace and make-up, I mean, but she looked normal. She has a great smile. But she's gay? Guess a person never can tell. What's the difference between a superdyke and an ordinary dyke? Why was she talking to me? I'm not gay. I don't look gay. I have a boyfriend. What makes her think she can go around assuming things like that? Jesus Christ.

* * * * *

The poetic types welcomed Daniel back with arms wide open. They held meetings of their Poet Laureate Club in the apartment, and would sit and drink and talk, talk, talk for hours.

"It's so sad. I mean, she takes off her pants, lays down and they scrape a little piece of gook out of her that was our baby."

"Ah, hell, Drake, she was nothing but a life support system for a pussy anyway." Kevin chugged the wine from the bottle, some of it dribbling out of the corner of his mouth and into his goatee. He was drunk, again.

"I don't have to listen to this. I'm going to bed," I said quietly to Daniel, who was sitting on the floor by the big chair I was in. I was sick of this subject and the smell of pot, patchouli, and b.o.

"But it was still my baby. I should've had more to do with it than paying for the abortion."

"You did. She got pregnant." I stood up. Four in the morning and everyone else had staggered home except them. Drake was okay. At least he'd make coffee in the morning and empty the ashtrays.

"I heard you met Cady Baird," Kevin said.

I nodded.

"She's in my Honors Philosophy class. Keeps bringing in all her lesbo shit. Buckrand loves it, he's got to be a closet case. Hey, what do you two use to keep the babies away —" He slid his finger in his mouth and slowly pulled it out, "the oral method?"

I'll bet your dick is only that big, you bastard. "Good night." I kissed Daniel on the top of his head.

He was staring at the floor and mumbled some answer.

"What?" Kevin asked.

Daniel stared him in the face. "I said, Ames can't have kids. She can't get pregnant."

That's none of their fucking concern, Daniel, not at all. It ran through my head, swinging back and forth like a rocking chair with each step down the hall.

55

* * * * *

"That it for today?" I asked the guy across the counter. He shook his head, tossed some money at me and crammed the candy bars in his pocket. They'd probably melt by the time he got around to eating them, it being so hot. And humid. Fucking great plains turn into a big green frying pan in the summer.

"Hi," Cady Baird said, grinning at me.

Silence lay between us like a dead thing. I stepped on my toe, under the counter where she couldn't see it. "Hi," I managed.

"Aren't you going to ring me up?"

"Oh. Yeah." I said, noticing the book in front of me. "Four-twenty."

She gave me a five. I gave her the change.

"Need a bag?"

Shaking her head, she stepped away toward the door, then turned back. "Could I get this gift-wrapped?"

"Can you wait a second?"

She nodded, her hair splashing over the front of her shirt like thick brush strokes of deep red paint.

I ran to the back room. Marielle was sitting there, smoking one of my cigarettes and talking on the phone. I held up the book and pointed to the wrap table. She tried to ignore me but gave up since I was being such a pest.

"Do it yourself," she hissed.

I glanced out the door. Nobody else was in the store but Cady, busy looking at magazines on the rack. Fast as I could I cut and folded and taped, even added a nice pink bow on top.

"Here you go." I set the package on the counter.

"How much?"

I shrugged. "Nothing." The bags under the counter were sure in need of straightening. I started doing it right then.

"You're sure?"

I nodded. A slow burn was itching at the edges of my face.

"Thank you. What a nice gesture." She pushed the wrapped book at me. "Here. For you."

Sitting in the Student Center ready to go back to the apartment, I passed the book from hand to hand, knowing I should find her and give it back till I finally ripped a little piece of the corner off. Not too much, but enough to ruin the wrap job.

"What the hell," I said and tore it open.

stills

Slushy gray mud that shows up only in November. One look out the window is enough. The sky is the color of asphalt, a sidewalk without dividers or chalk-drawn hopscotch marks.

Damn phone rings. Sorry this isn't the Admittance Office. We don't admit anything here. I toss the phone back. It lands plastic and plastic in a perfect fit.

The scrapbook on the floor is spread open to a blank page. I pull it over, another edge tears all crooked and hairy the way construction paper does. Not taking very good care of this book. I lost Sylvia's picture somewhere, and when I taped Joanna Nobody next to Jessie, her picture got scraped away to white in the corners. Poor Jo Nobody. The rest of the book, Jessie Cassandra Walker's memories glued across ten by sixteen inch pages, is disintegrating in slivers from me going through it over and over. I'm so young here. I don't remember many of the photographs. The first thing I can remember is the slant of the sunlight on the wall in my bedroom and how the bars of my crib cut it sideways every morning. I can remember those last days with Jess when she spoke so slowly as if each word was a fish she had to catch with her bare hands. Her breath smelled like dust, like coal that's finally been touched by the sun and wind. I thought she'd've smelled like rotting or blood or sweat, but it was none of those live things. She smelled like the gray color she'd become.

I turn to the beginning. I've tried looking at the pictures from every which way — back to front, upside down, even flipped the scrapbook to begin at whatever page it opens to, always the one with me singing in the snow because I cracked the glue binding by stepping on it. But order doesn't matter, I decided. Pictures hold pieces of time and time is fucked. Rip Van Winkle was wrong — go to sleep for years and when you wake up, nothing's different, just the same getting out of one shithole to fall into another. That's all there is in this book, slices of minutes held in by black corners.

An empty milk container lies next to the book on the floor. I stare at the yellow and green cow on the side. The yellow ink somehow got away from the picture, so the cow's either really fat or it has a strange shadow.

My tongue is flat and fuzzy like a piece of carpet. At least I should think about going to class. I haven't been anywhere but the liquor store for a week. The grocery cart that holds my laundry is overflowing with clothes like the rest of the room. There must be half a foot of shit on the floor, mostly jeans and shirts and smelly towels.

I yank out my favorite pair of jeans. They're comfortable, these jeans. They're ripped out at the knees.

Mine always rip at the knees. I had a friend whose jeans always tore right below the back pockets. This pair is faded almost to white and doesn't smell as bad as some of the others.

It's Thursday. I wonder what time it is. I must be late for class because there isn't any more noise in the hall. I don't have a clock since Daniel took it along with everything else and I'm living in a postage-stamp sized room in the dorms. I think I'm really late. Maybe I'll go to the zoo instead. I like the monkey island the best, but only if I'm standing upwind.

Damn him to hell

* * * * *

I tried to pull a sweater over my backpack as I walked to the can. I saw in the mirror that I'd guessed right about my hair; it was standing practically on end. Ducking my head under a faucet, I turned on the water, shocked from the coldness. I got the sweater on right and let the water drip into my collar as I half-combed and half-shoved my hair into place.

"What time is it?" I asked some girl standing in the hall. I wasn't too late for Feminist Theory class. I jogged across campus, partly because I can't notice anything when I hurry and partly from the cold drizzle seeping into my clothes.

The room was dark. I tried to slip in unnoticed, so of course everybody waiting for the movie to start gaped as I made my way to my usual seat in the very back. McClure, the Teaching Assistant, flipped the projector on soon as I sat down.

There was no title, just a typed statement about the film being made by a women's collective and other bullshit. It looked pretty low-budget, grainy black and white like it'd been shot through a lens covered with sand. At first I thought it was some artsy-fartsy silent flick with all still photographs till the speaker snapped and cracked, waking me up if no one else. McClure had finally figured out which button was for volume.

A woman's voice spoke. Every eighteen seconds a woman is beaten. Every four minutes a woman is raped.

Pictures flashed on the screen, girls smiling and looking pretty, then bodies. Knifed or tortured or shot or strangled or left to suffocate underground, in the trunk of a car or in a garbage bag like the eight-year-old found at a garbage dump.

Shit, shit, I do not want to see this.

An old face, so old it could've been either female or male, wrinkled and close-eyed, mouth open. Scared into a heart attack, the voice said, that didn't stop the guy even though she was dead. Another little girl, father in jail and her body covered with cigarette burns.

My body felt too big for the desk. Then too big for the room. I can't watch this.

The voice went on and on, telling of women who lived but couldn't look at the camera. Some were still married to the men who had raped them, beat them, crippled them.

The screen went black except for white lines from scratches in the film.

More pictures, this time of men hiding their faces from the cameras, mug shots, high school pictures, snapshots from family picnics, the men who'd done these things. Some went to jail, some didn't, some went to mental institutions to be freed in months.

"McClure, turn the projector off," Rhys Dawson said over the voice.

64

The room went dark for a moment. The fluorescent lights came on and I sat up, muscles too tight for my skin, knees bouncing up and down, up and down, making the desk squeak in time.

"Amory?"

I looked at Rhys. A crease appeared between her eyebrows, something I'd never seen before.

"Would you please open the windows behind you?"

I got up. I didn't even know she knew my name. The windows slid open easily. The drizzle had turned into the beginnings of a real storm. The trees were black from too much water in the bark already, and the fallen leaves were shoved flat against the mud and the grass, the rain popping against them like small drums. I took a deep breath and went back.

"Get out a piece of paper, everyone." She paused as we all dug through bookbags and notebooks. "I want you to write a reaction," she began, stepping across the front of the room with her hands clasped in front and her thumbs together like an L. "I know this is difficult, but your reaction is valuable and I want you to put it into words. McClure and I are going to leave the room and I want you to write down what you are feeling. Don't theorize, don't philosophize. Just write."

She stopped and faced us, balancing on one leg and letting the palm of her hand bounce lightly on the top of her thigh. "When you've finished, take a deep breath, find a place within yourself, some kind of sanctuary, and think about what you just saw."

I looked at my blank sheet, clicking my pen in and out, in and out. My hand moved across the sheet of paper but nothing filled it. Try to explain the fear of having a nightmare becoming a day mare, a fear of knives and not being able to run. Fear of time slipping away like water

65

through my open hand and Jessie dragging me back to when the dream began. Then McClure was standing over me, waiting. I skated through anger and sadness and a strange twisted empty feeling of loss till things fell from my hand onto the page. I gave it to her without reading it.

Rhys leaned into the podium, her hands gripping the edges.

"I want to face the horror of rape before discussing it in terms of feminist theory. There is a beginning premise for this discussion: one's experience is the ultimate measure of reality. Think about what you are feeling —" She peered around the room at us, "and what you have lived through. That is the screen on which to throw the images society forces on us. Oppression is the denial of someone's experience for the sake of maintaining the status quo."

The room went silent, except for the scribbling of pens as Rhys's disciples recorded her pearls of wisdom. Jessie had a saying about throwing words to pigs: it was a waste of time since they couldn't hear for the noise from their eating of everything in sight.

She scanned the room again and took a deep breath I could hear all the way in back and I wondered if everybody wrote that down, too. "What shall we do with rapists?"

I looked down at my desk. M.H. loves T.C. Isn't that nice? It fit with the carvings and grains already in the wood. Jess also used to say fools' names and fools' faces should not be seen in public places. She'd repeat it every time we'd drive past a bridge on a side where people hung over the railing to scribble their names with a can of paint and a broom. Rapists. Fools. Love and people not knowing what they're talking about. Shit. What am I doing here?

"But rape is how men keep women in their places and we have to retaliate," somebody said, jerking me back to class.

A strong, clear voice filled the room, the words clean and clipped and neat: "I agree that rape is a means to an end, but I can't advocate violence."

"Then, Cady, what should we do with men who rape?"

"I don't know." Cady Baird's voice fell a little. "My gut reaction is a little too much even for me, which is why I'm glad I'm not ruled by gut reactions. Rape is one means for men to secure power, but I think rape and similar crimes are symptoms of a larger problem."

"Rape is the larger problem," another woman half-shouted. "Men think they have the right to take what they want. We should castrate them. Look what they do to us!" She crossed her arms.

Words, words, the way they threw them at each other reminded me of how Tad Sudheimer and I'd have rock fights; both of us would grab a handful of gravel and whale it so hard we'd both miss. I raised my hand quick enough to be mistaken for a twitch.

"Get back to the question. Go ahead, Amory."

My stomach tightened. I'd never said nothing in here before, especially not to the cross-armed woman looking mad as hell. "You can't assume you can stop some guy from hurting people by chopping his balls off. You said yourself that a guy thinks he can do whatever he wants. Cut off his dick and that's not going to change anything but the way he walks."

She only glared at me.

"That's a very good point," Rhys jumped in. "Understanding rape as a crime of violence, not a sex crime. Both you and Cady are bringing in the dynamics of society and how rape is a symptom as well as a problem. But my original question remains, Amory: what are we to do with men who rape?"

"I can't answer that," I said, my voice flapping against my throat like a moth with its wings stuck. Rhys watched me. Cady Baird watched me. Everybody in the fucking room was staring. My eyes followed my arms to where my hands dropped over the edge of my desk. "Maybe we'll never know what to do with them."

Rhys was still listening. She wasn't going to let me get by with that.

"Maybe we got to hang onto some healthy paranoia," I offered, trying to remember what I read, "and stop getting into places where it's either fight or fuck. Maybe we got to quit being embarrassed about making noise when we get into a crummy situation."

"Doesn't that leave the responsibility for safe streets and safe places to live to potential victims, even though those are our rights?" Cady pointed out.

"Women don't have rights in the real world," the cross-armed woman broke in, still mean and mad-looking.

"How are we going to get them?" Cady asked.

"Not by cutting some guy's nuts off," I answered.

"I think," Rhys stated, "that we better end this right here. We're on the right track, but I want everyone to think about it and read the chapters for the next class."

I zipped my backpack shut and stood up.

"Amory? Could you wait?" I heard Rhys from the front of the room. "It will only take a minute."

I stopped inside the door.

Cady Baird stood in the middle of the room. "Just to remind you, at seven tonight the Ova Dance Collective will be performing in the Fine Arts Lounge," she announced. "Admission is free, so I hope to see you there." All finished, she walked up to me, half-staring and half-smiling. "Effortlessly beautiful and intelligent, too. Are you going to their performance?"

I shook my head.

"Well, since I won't have the chance to charm you tonight, how about a cup of coffee now?"

I took a deep breath. Goddamn she had a way of saying all the wrong things. "Rhys wants to talk to me."

"After? I can meet you." She grinned, cocky and full of herself. "I don't bite, Amory, at least not in public. What do you say?"

"What the hell." I blushed. "All right." I've always been a sucker for redheads.

"I'll be waiting at the end of the hall." As she walked away I noticed she had three earrings in her left ear.

People stood around the room waiting to see if they could help Rhys. They were always floating around at the end of class or near her office. The only one who ever seemed to be of much help was McClure, who was now leaning against the front of the podium, her oversized vest hanging wide enough to read Everybody is Somebody in Snellville on her T-shirt. She had on canvas tennis shoes with big rubber toes, the kind we used to call bumpers when I was a kid, and she had a funny tooth in front, chipped at the bottom like a quarter moon as if she got hit in the face playing dodge ball in third grade. She was kind of nice looking, though she was serious all the time. Daniel would say she was a member of the earth mother-sky father gang.

"You want me for something?"

"Uh huh." Rhys started shoveling papers into her briefcase. "Would you like to go over to the Center, maybe get something to eat?"

"Cady Baird is waiting for me. I think she wants to keep fighting."

"I don't doubt it," McClure broke in. "Cady B. is always looking for a good fight."

And that ain't all. "You can come along, if you like," I suggested. "We're just going for coffee."

"You wouldn't mind?" Rhys looked up from what she was doing.

"Am I in a lot of trouble?"

Her briefcase was all leather, even the clasps were leather clasps instead of metal locks. "Not with me."

"Then it's okay. You too, McClure."

McClure fastened the last snap on her camouflage poncho. "I'd love to."

Rhys got into her raincoat. Jessie was always saying how women can never carry their age. I always thought that was stupid, who wants to look like a sixteen-year-old when she's forty-five? Rhys Dawson looked exactly as old as she was with her black hair streaked with shiny silver and her face brown from the sun. Maybe if I'm careful I can look that great.

"How's work these days?" Rhys asked. "Getting along better with Marielle?"

"A lot better. I quit."

Cady was standing at the end of the hall talking to someone as we walked towards her. "Hi," she said when we were within hearing distance. "This is Joe Don Barrett, my roommate."

"Hello," he said, sticking his hand out to McClure.

"I'm McClure Thomas."

"I think we've met before."

"At Angel's show."

"That's right," he nodded. "And she didn't bother to introduce us. She's a wonderful artist but has the

70

manners of a baboon." His voice was soft, each word slipping into the one ahead of it.

"Hello, Joe Don. I'm Rhys Dawson."

He flashed her a dazzling smile. He was extremely good-looking. "Hi."

"Amory Walker."

"So you're Amory."

I expected his hand to be soft like an old woman's, but it was strong and calloused as if he were a sailor always working ropes.

"Well, doll," he said to Cady, "I'll see you tonight. Dinner will be ready at seven."

"Fabulous." She gave him a hug and turned back. "Going to join us for coffee?"

"We've decided on it," McClure answered.

"Great. Fascism lives," Cady said, leading the way.

We walked out into the clearing day and over to the Center. Rhys and Cady talked non-stop about some project or another as we crowded around a small circular table near a window. I tried to listen, tried to look interested, but pretty soon the only thing that could hold my attention was the grease rainbow floating on the top of my coffee.

I looked up to find McClure watching me. Shit, busted looking bored in the middle of the conversation.

"Dull, aren't they?" she asked, quiet enough so they couldn't hear.

"Uh huh," I said, still embarrassed.

"You really said some good things today."

I pushed my thumbnail into the styrofoam cup, making an indent that looked like a crescent moon. "Don't think what I said went anywhere."

"The whole discussion didn't seem to be going anywhere, don't worry. Rhys had a feeling that was going to happen. It's hard to talk about rape when everything inside you is churning."

"I guess." I watched the rainbow, then glanced back up.

"I've been wondering, maybe it's none of my business, but, uh, is everything okay?"

"What do you mean?" My voice was even.

"I know Daniel Jacobson." She looked right at me.

The buzzing on the other side of the table stopped and the other two stared as well. There was a rough spot on the inside of my cheek from me chewing on it all the time.

"I haven't seen you in class for a while." She spoke delicately, as if afraid of breaking something.

"You know Daniel?" I punched another crescent into the side of my cup and looked at her.

She nodded.

"Then you know there's nothing to worry about." I shrugged and gulped some coffee. It was gritty like sand against my teeth.

"Is there something else —" Rhys broke in from the other side of the table. I saw the line between her eyes come back.

"No."

Rhys and McClure glanced at each other then at me as silence slipped over the table. I settled into my chair and looked at McClure, her eyes slate gray and direct. I hope I never have to tell her a lie.

"Drink your coffee." Cady smiled suddenly. "The Inquisition is over. Almost."

"Great. Time for the whips and chains?"

"No. Just conversation. Where did you get your name?"

"I don't know."

"No one ever told you?"

"Never had the chance to ask. And if my Aunt Jessie knew, she wasn't telling."

"Who's she?"

"She wasn't really my aunt. She just called herself that." The last of my coffee was lukewarm.

"Why don't you ask her?"

"I'll hold a seance next week to do just that." I stared at her. Somehow I got the feeling of being in biology lab and I was the one being dissected. I pushed the red anger back. Cady was just trying to be friendly, just talking. "You know, though, I once found a book, a hardback copy of *This Side of Paradise*."

"By F. Scott Fitzgerald," McClure broke in.

"Yeah. Anyway, Jess had it stashed away in the top drawer of her nightstand. The main character was a guy named Amory Blaine. So I usually tell people my name came from that book. Makes them think I came from somewhere." I smiled at Cady and she smiled back, some of the tenseness slipping away. "Lots of people call me Ames or Amy."

"What do you want to be called?" asked McClure.

"I don't mind Ames, but I hate Amy. Makes me sound like a little girl."

"You didn't like being a little girl?"

I turned to answer Cady. "Hell, no. Took me years to get out of that stage."

"Did you get that scar when you were little?"

Which one, I almost asked. Damn, she doesn't have x-ray vision. I put my hand to the small white scar and gave her a big grin. "That's none of your fucking business."

McClure shifted in her chair and muffled a giggle in her coffee cup. Rhys's hand was over her mouth, I think over a smile threatening to escape.

"It happened a long time ago," I said, feeling like I'd rebuilt my fences and she wasn't going to go wandering in my backyard again, "and it wasn't no ride on a pink chicken."

McClure cracked up and so did Rhys even though it wasn't that funny.

"A pink chicken?" This time Cady's eyebrow slid up. "Where did you hear that?"

"Jessie'd say shit like that all the time. Hey, anybody want another cup of coffee?"

McClure pulled out her pocket watch. "Dammit, I'm late." She scooped up her bright orange backpack.

Rhys stood up and gave her a hug.

"I'm leaving, too," she said as McClure walked away. "This day has been too long to be believed." She patted Cady on the shoulder, gave me a little wave and followed McClure.

"I like Rhys," I said.

"I do, too. She's great."

"She doesn't babble on and on about useless shit."

Cady nodded. "You know what sucks? People are always turning her into a symbol instead of letting her be a person. If they'd quit being so uptight about her being a dyke, they'd see an absolutely brilliant and very fragile woman."

"People get upset when they find out?"

"Find out what?"

"That Rhys and you are gay."

"Lesbian, you mean?" She shook her head. "Not really. The hardest part is dealing with it in your own head. Why? Thinking of switching?" She looked like a kid who never got caught in the cookie jar.

"You make it sound like changing cigarettes."

74

"I hope not. It's a thousand times more fun."

I snuck a quick look around to make sure no one was listening.

"When did you stop working at the bookstore?"

The question surprised me. I thought I was going to get a lesbian recruitment speech. "Back in June. I'm a full-time student again."

"You like it better?"

"For now. Isn't exactly what I thought it would be."

"Is anything what anybody thought it was going to be?"

"Gee, you sound so grown up."

She bit her lip. "Guess that's twice in less than half an hour I made a fool of myself."

"You guessed right."

"I didn't mean to be patronizing."

"You mean matronizing?"

"You sound like Jill."

" 'Liberate our language.' Makes it sound like stealing. Like I liberated a case of beer from the back of a truck."

"Does, doesn't it?" Cady chuckled. "So what do you do then?"

"Write. I want to be a writer. I think."

"You think?"

"Yeah." I twisted in my chair. "I'm not like you or McClure or any of those gir— women in class. I'm only at the thinking stage of things."

"Don't let their insecurity stop you from doing your work."

"It doesn't. It's just —" I stopped.

"Yeah?"

"Everybody here thinks you have to read everything ever written to have something to say. They want people all to sound the same on the page."

"I don't think that." The gold of her earrings flashed as the sun got through the clouds and into the windows. "Why do you want to write?"

"Economics, baby. If I can't buy a pen and some paper, I'll liberate them."

She waited.

"I think it's mostly because words can do things people can't. They're not sacred things, though plenty of people kill people over them." I tugged my hair as she watched me. "What do you do?"

"Political bullshit. Everything I do is political bullshit." Cady sat up like she'd been shaken awake and stared past me at the doors.

"You like it?"

"Wouldn't do it if I didn't. I love being the center of attention."

"What are you looking at?" I craned my neck but missed it.

"I thought it was George Hammerstand. You know George, don't you?"

I shook my head. "I don't know many people around here. Not exactly my type."

"Not mine, either." She sipped her coffee. "So, what do you think of this feminist theory class?"

"Sometimes I learn things, sometimes I don't. A lot of it is mighty strange and a lot of it is horsecrap that I could do without."

"Like rape?" she asked.

"Like rape."

"Who couldn't?"

We sat quiet for awhile, watching the Center empty of people. I got some more coffee, treating her to another huge cup.

"I'm sorry I asked about your scar."

"Doesn't matter." My shoulders twitched like I just missed getting hit in the back. "I'm sorry I got so snotty about it." It got awful hard to look at her right then. "I got your book. The one you gave me last spring, I mean."

"Did you read it?"

"I tried. I started but then everything started freaking out."

"Will you read it now?"

"Maybe." I stared at the tile floor. "Maybe."

"We could talk about it, if you want."

I looked up at her again. "Can I ask you something?"

"You bet."

I cleared my throat. "Remember when we met? On the steps?"

"Yeah?"

"What's the difference between you saying what you said and some jerk guy saying it?"

"Haven't you ever wanted to start a conversation with someone?"

"That wasn't what you were trying to do."

"Maybe not." Cady looked at her coffee. "In which case that makes me just another one of the idiots."

I pulled a cigarette out and tapped it against the pack. "No. You're an unusual idiot."

"Thanks. Good to know I'm not of the common garden variety." She got that same little kid grin on her face as before, then sipped her coffee, holding the cup in two hands like she was going to throw a football. "Everybody is always telling me I need to learn about patience," she said, more to herself than me. "You know, Amory," she said, grinning at me now all upbeat, "your reputation is getting cracked further and further open every second you sit here with me."

"Reputation? I didn't even know I had one." Which was the truth. People around here are too busy either shoveling or avoiding shit to take a good look around.

"But you do. And it's getting smashed to bits. Imagine Daniel Jacobson's ex-girlfriend, who became his ex through mysterious circumstances, sitting in the middle of the Chase University Student Center drinking coffee with a notorious dyke and enjoying herself. You are enjoying yourself, aren't you?"

"You're okay for a girl." I lit up for the first time that day.

"Thoroughly enjoying herself. Stay tuned for the next piece of the puzzle."

"You should go to Hollywood and be in the fucking movies, Cady." I rolled my eyes, a last influence of Daniel. "The circumstances weren't that big a mystery, anyway. He's an asshole and I got sick of it. Period."

"That I believe."

"You know him?"

"Uh huh. But I don't want to talk about him. I want to talk about you."

"I'm not very good food for conversation."

"Oh, I don't know. I'll bet you're delicious."

"Why don't we talk about you instead? Where do you come from, how did you get your name, and do you have any scars you'd like to talk about?"

She put her hands up in self-defense. "Okay, okay, I admit it. I'm incorrigible."

"You're nosy."

"At least I'm woman enough to admit it."

"That's true."

"Will you forgive me and say we'll be friends anyway?"

I paused to consider it. "I suppose I could give it a shot."

We shook hands over coffee and a burning cigarette.

I picked up my cup. "I think I really was named after that guy in the book," I said over the rim.

"The real question, Amory," she smiled, this time slow and gentle, "is which side of paradise are you on?"

*****

"Amory, wait a minute!"

I heard the shout from behind. Turning, I saw McClure running down the hall, practically dropping everything.

"Jesus, you ran out of there so fast I thought you were going to throw up."

"I just wanted to get outside." The classroom walls had moved too close again, closer than the other day even, seemed to touch my skin as everybody argued and fought over something they knew nothing about. I walked on, McClure half a step behind, bouncing books and papers to get them going in the same direction.

"I wanted to tell you that I read your reaction paper."

I stopped dead in the middle of the doorway.

"It's one of the best pieces of poetry I've ever read."

I walked out. "It ain't poetry."

"Then what would you call it?"

"It's junk I scratched down from my head after seeing pictures of dead women and beat-up women and women too ashamed to look up." My voice was rough, like stones were weighing down the words.

79

"Amory, it's poetry." She said it the same way she'd say the world was round or that my shoes were untied. McClure grabbed my arm and stepped in front of me. "It's a poem, Ames. It needs work, but it has power in it. Poetry is in the voice of the work, and most people don't find it because they don't listen. Most people want easy stuff to read, all perfectly true, perfectly vague, and perfectly meaningless." She stared at me as if I'd taken off a mask just this very second. "I'd like to see some more. Will you let me?"

I stepped around her.

"Amory."

I stopped again.

"I'm not going to steal your words. I like this poem that slipped from your hand. I don't know if it was an accident, but I'd like to find out."

I spun on my heel to face her. "Why? Why the fuck —" I couldn't finish.

She took a deep breath, looking at the ground. Her head bobbed up and down as if she were nodding yes to a thousand of her own questions, then she looked up. "Because."

*****

McClure could give pieces of herself away like somebody else's china. She brought me books to read, food to eat, even once offered me her raincoat during an autumn storm. I read and ate, and told her thanks but no thanks for the raincoat because she has weird taste in clothes. Coffee and cigarettes after class with her became a habit, like brushing my teeth.

"Poor crazy Virginia Woolf. Filled her pockets full of rocks and tried to walk on water." She shook her head sadly as if it'd happened the day before yesterday.

"That's what she gets for trying to play Jesus," I said. "Did you ever think about trying to kill yourself?"

"What a depressing topic, Ames." She picked up her cup of tea and thought about it. "Yeah, I did, come to think of it. Strictly for poetic convention, I was never serious about it."

"Serious about what? Hi, buddy." Cady threw her backpack on the table and brushed snow out of her scarf. I smiled at her. She looked great, her cheeks pink from the cold and her eyes shining.

"Amory just asked if I ever thought about jumping in a manhole and committing sewercide."

"Let me get Joe Don. He loves to talk about sex. May I have a cigarette?"

I tossed her the pack, then flicked the matchbook so it skidded across the table, sliding to a stop right on the edge. "Two points."

She lit her cigarette and threw the matches back. "Go for a goal," she said, her fingers up to make goal posts.

"I suck at this." I snapped the matchbook. It flipped over Cady's head and landed on some kid's book on the table behind us. He sort of sneered and threw the matches back. "Fuck you, bubblehead," I muttered.

"Did you ever think about it, Ames?"

"You bet. But I always figured there were too many goddamn things against me as it was. Your turn, Baird." I tossed the matches and put my hands up.

"Like what?" she asked instead of going for a goal.

81

"Just stuff." Why not tell them about getting hit in the back with a beer bottle. Tell them about falling face down in the gravel road because it hurt so much. Tell them about the laughing and the names as the car roared away. "How about you, Cady? Did you ever want to commit the big S?"

Cady got real quiet, moving only every now and then to the ashtray. "I have a little brother. My god, he's twelve now. Duncan MacKeon Baird. My little brother. He has the most beautiful gray-green eyes I have ever seen, clear like the stained glass windows in a church, you know? Like those windows in the morning."

She blew a perfect smoke ring and I smiled. I'd been trying to teach her how for two weeks.

"He's autistic. He's such an awkward kid, a real klutz. My dad calls him Charlie Chaplin because they walk the same, and he's always telling Duncan what to do in one word, like a dog. No, Duncan. Stay, Duncan. Sit, Duncan. The only time he'll talk to him in complete sentences is when he's reading Duncan a short story to put him to sleep. But eight, no, yeah, eight years ago when they thought my mom wouldn't be able to handle him because she'd been sick, they were going to put him away."

I watched her inhale, her green eyes getting white-washed by the gray light coming in the window as she stared at the snow.

"They actually did it. They took him somewhere for about a week and I thought he was never coming back. I wrote the note and planned how I would kill myself." Her voice trailed away with the smoke.

"What happened?" McClure asked gently.

"My mom brought him back. She couldn't stand him not being around." Cady sat up in her chair and smiled. "That's it, the only time I ever really gave it any serious

82

thought. Hey, I'm hungry. You want to get something to eat?"

We walked to the snack bar ignoring everybody but us.

* * * * *

I was never real good at making friends more than one at a time and Cady and McClure were almost bent on being different from each other. I was so busy watching them that the cold days walked into one another like jumbled Christmas shoppers, giving hours away as presents. A person gets spoiled by such things, pieces of time all glitter-wrapped and shiny.

Spring finally showed up, leaving dogshit defrosting on the grass alongside the rest of the trash. McClure gave me a list of books to read, some in the library and some at Juniper's bookstore. Juniper's was a lot like Daniel's bookstore except there was an upstairs and no Romance section. I found a lot of good books, cheap because they were old or somebody's three-year-old had crayoned all over the third chapter.

I was trying to catch up with all the feminists and a lot of their stuff didn't wash right with me. Jessie used to say how a person could like the singing except for the song and some of this got me feeling like that. It was a good thing Cady was there. She understood most of it, liked some of it, and believed none of it.

McClure's smart but Cady's quicker. She could take people apart with their own words while they sat there watching. When things would get real bad in class she'd lean on her elbow, stare at somebody from across the room, and say, Well, what are you going to do about it? Sometimes they'd get mad about it, but I guess she figured they could get glad in the same pants they got mad in. After she'd piss somebody off, she'd sit back and comb her fingers through her hair, the red glinting in the afternoon sunlight that shone through the windows.

* * * * *

McClure's house isn't too far from the dorm. I walked over, my jean jacket getting its first wearing. Today had been the first spring day and I still felt warm from the sun, even though it was night and the streetlights were swapping my shadow every half-block. Down the avenue a couple of blocks and two houses on the left after the stop sign. I'd been to McClure's a couple of times but I always had to get directions.

My boots sounded hollow as I walked across the cobblestones of the park. This was the strangest park I'd ever seen, with a monument in the middle and flowers trying to grow around the broken glass at the base. I think it was once a street divider but they closed the road except to people on foot and bikes.

I turned the corner onto her street. A low black Triumph slid into a parking place and whoever was driving slipped out and headed for the party. A second later a Datsun 300ZX pulled up, metallic puke-orange by the fluorescent streetlights. The driver had hair down to his ass and didn't look like any of the other men McClure knew, the ones who stay in the library so long their skin looks bleached. He sort of shoved me on the way up the walk to the door.

"Shithead," I said, loud enough so he could hear it though he pretended not to. Stuff like that usually doesn't bother me, but he had no right nor reason, there was plenty of room. I must be reading too much feminism stuff.

He didn't ring the doorbell. I didn't either, but followed him up the stairs. McClure had the top of this huge motherfucking house with high ceilings and wood floors. It was a nice place, not overdone, and looked like she actually thought about where she wanted to put something before sitting it down. Her roommate said he didn't give a flying fuck what she did with the inside, so she hung up pictures signed by the people who painted them, a beaded curtain between the dining room and the living room, and plants everywhere. There were bookshelves that stretched the whole way down the wall to an elephant's foot trashcan she'd found at a garage sale that sat next to the front door. McClure's been living alone since Vince moved out, leaving his blender and his stereo when he went to Africa.

The party was pretty quiet when I walked in the door. McClure saw me and came over to give me a hug and a kiss before taking my jacket and sailing away with it, barely giving me time to get my cigarettes. She was back in two seconds with another hug and a beer.

"You look great," I said, taking the cold can. She did. Her dark hair was brushed into a single braid and her cheeks were flushed because of the gross awful wine she drinks. She looked softer somehow. Maybe it was the candlelight. Maybe it was her clothes. She had on the kind of dress people on Grecian urns wear — long and pleated with a belt around her hips. Instead of being white, it was a nut-brown, the same shade I tan if I lie in the sun all summer long. "Snappy outfit."

McClure glanced down. "Thank you. People are surprised. I guess they don't think I'm the dress type."

"Well, I like it."

"I'm glad." She touched my arm lightly. "I'm glad you're here. We'll talk later, okay?"

I stood just inside the doorway, sipping my beer and looking around. There were more people than the noise would let on, sitting on the couch or leaning against the big pillows, and what seemed like a million candles, some in holders and some resting on saucers or tinfoil, scattered all over the room. The little flames flickered every now and then as a small cluster of people would laugh. It wasn't the loud braying I heard at other college parties where everyone got drunk and watched everybody else throw up or pass out.

"Hi." A small woman stood next to me, ready for conversation, and looking like an ad for Guatemalan clothing. "How are you doing, Amory? It's nice to see you."

"Doing all right, Jill."

"I want to thank you for putting up my posters."

I searched her face to see if she was lying or not. She'd left a stack of her concert posters for me and McClure to hang so we papered the women's can on the first floor of the Admin Building. "You play a lot?"

"As much as I can. I'd like to go big time, but the parental units aren't too happy about that."

I checked out the room trying to see if Cady had shown up.

"What do you want to do after you graduate?"

"Write. I'm a writer." McClure had moved her Georgia O'Keeffe poster from above the bookshelves and had some weird woven thing on the wall instead.

"That's great. What kind of writing?"

"Any kind where I get to lie and tell the truth at the same time." I downed half my beer while standing there.

"Does your family give you a hard time?"

"Nobody gives a fuck."

"Oh, that's right, your parents are dead."

I noticed she wasn't very tall, stood only to my shoulder and had hair curlier than mine. Her eyes seemed huge since she was looking up, and she had a jawline a giraffe would kill for. I walked over to the end of the sofa to sit on the floor. She walked behind, jabbering about L.A. cool. "What kind of music do you play?" I asked to keep her busy as she settled against the wall with a cushion propped up behind her.

"All kinds. Blues, folk. I've been focusing a lot on women's music lately. I'd love to work in that kind of environment. It has a lot of political and artistic power, don't you think?"

"Uh huh," I muttered into the can. What the fuck is women's music?

"Hi." Cady appeared, standing above me in the candlelight.

I smiled, resting the now-empty beer can on my knee.

She sat across from me. "What's going on over here?"

"Talking about music. I'm going to get a drink," Jill said. "Do you want anything?"

I held up my beer. Cady shook her head.

"Will you save my place?" she said to me, her face practically on mine.

"Till hell is a frigidaire dealership," I lied.

Cady watched as Jill walked the long hall to the kitchen. "Were you really talking about music or did she lecture and you nod at all the right places?"

I touched her nose with the tip of my finger. "Bingo."

"I thought so." Her face shifted, turning sad even though she was smiling. "What's it like in Sterling, Ames?"

All the times we sat shooting the shit and she's never asked me this. I shrugged. "Why?"

"I've just been thinking."

87

"About what? Come on. You can tell me."

It was her turn to shrug. "Home. Not having one."

"You have a home."

"But I don't belong anywhere, you know? My parents moved again, my brother is in a special school and probably won't even remember me. It feels all so scattered. See, I never had a hometown. At least you have Sterling."

I laughed short and sharp and pulled out a cigarette. "Have Sterling? Nobody has Sterling. It has you." My stomach started to hurt as I lit up. "In my hometown, there are the niggers, the white trash, and the cream that rises above it all." I held the smoke way down, looking over the titles on the bookshelves. McClure never let her books gather dust, not from being cleanly, but from re-reading everything. "In Sterling, a girl gets married to the guy she dated and let fuck her since eighth grade and he goes to work in the mines and she has nine zillion kids and a job where the minimum wage glaze moves into her face and the only thing she can think of is the next day off. Nothing great about having a hometown."

"But it's a home, Amory. And it's yours."

"A home does cling to you. Like dirt you can't get out of your skin."

"And that's all Sterling is?"

I nodded.

"Do you have a home now?" she asked.

"Got no people, but I've a new place to live. The rest will come when it's due."

"But what is the rest, Amory? I've been wondering."

I dragged on my cigarette, pulling smoke deep. "I don't know, Cady." Jill touched my shoulder with a cold can and sat down. I opened it, the pressure spraying my fingers with beer.

"What are you talking about?" Jill asked.

"Sterling, West Virginia. Ames's home town," Cady quickly answered.

"I had the bad luck of growing up there." I drank some more beer and smoked in the sharp silence. Cady was looking at me, trying to hold onto my eyes long enough to figure out what I was thinking. "And I'm never going back."

"Why not?" Jill spoke again.

"Because everyone hates anyone who's a different color and they tell little girls they're only worth as much as the men they're with." Every muscle seemed part of some crazy orchestra trying to tune up to a tone-deaf bassoon player.

"And you want more." Cady's eyes kept searching mine, looking for something that I didn't want to give up. "Like what?"

"Like what?" How to admit I didn't have the faintest notion. "I don't know." I struggled. "Just something better. Something more. Something bigger than just being proud of things I didn't do."

"You make me sick,"shrilled through the room. Cady and I looked over. I recognized the guy immediately. He'd timed his point perfect; the Rolling Stones album on the stereo was in need of being turned over.

"You sit here in your downwardly-mobile designer clothes, warm and educated, and bitch about being broke. There are people starving to death." His hands chopped through the air like he could cut all the world's problems in half just by doing that. With each jerk of his elbow the strung beads swung and clacked into one another.

"What the hell?" Cady said softly over her shoulder.

"Cheap thrills in the monkey house," I said back, leaning towards her. I knew she heard because she nodded.

"You don't know what poverty is."

"Wait a minute, Rocky," McClure said, never needing to shout to be heard. "That's not the point."

He cut her off. "You're a fake, McClure, a fucking hypocrite. You and your social justice."

Cady was up in a second, ready for a good fight. "You righteous prick, think you know it all because you got your hair down to your ass."

"Leave it to a dyke to pick on something so meaningless," he spat.

"You're telling me it's meaningless," she shot back.

I got to my feet. "Rocky?" I took another drag and stepped around Cady. "That your name?"

"Who the fuck are you?" Now he was mad. I could almost see sparks coming off the ends of his righteous hair.

"I want to tell you your car is parked next to a fire hydrant. I'd hate to see you get a ticket, since you know so much about being poor and all."

I dropped my cigarette into my beer and it made a quiet hiss. "You know, Rocky," I said, very friendly as I swirled the beer around and around. "You could sell that Datsun and do some good things. There's a family I know that has no indoor plumbing, been using the same brick shithouse for generations. You want me to find their address for you?"

Finally feeling in tune like nothing was crossgrain to nothing, I spun on my heel and walked down the hall to the kitchen. I tossed the empty can into the box labeled Cans Only. The stereo was turned way up in the other room, Mick Jager screaming away as if to drown out the words with the music. I stood belly up to the counter leaning on my arms. My reflection in the black window above the sink had no face.

"Amory?"

I saw McClure in the glass, part of her hidden by the plants on the sill.

"Are you all right?"

Turning around, I nodded.

"I'm sorry."

"Why? You didn't do nothing. People shouldn't apologize when something ain't their fault." I pulled a cigarette out of my pack.

"Rocky's an asshole."

I lit a match, cupping it with one hand, the flame turning my skin pink and yellow. "Well," I said, "You can be as old as Methuselah and still be a fool."

She didn't smile. "He thinks he has great insight because he went to Nicaragua last fall."

"Yeah, and if I had his car and he had a feather up his ass, we'd both be tickled pink."

"I heard that," Cady said, walking into the room and not stopping till she stood right in front of me, close enough so I could see she had bits of brown in her green eyes. "Why don't we talk downstairs?"

I crossed my arms and cocked my head, eyes slitting from the smoke. "On one condition: we don't talk about poverty."

"It's a deal. McClure," she spoke over her shoulder, "I'm going to monopolize the jug of wine in your refrigerator and the room at the bottom of the stairs."

"Corkscrew's in the drawer with the forks," she said flatly, swinging a stare from me to Cady, then walking out to leave us alone.

91

"So," Cady asked, grabbing two glasses, "who's your favorite cartoon character?"

* * * * *

"I threw darts at him," I answered. Cady and I were in a small room by the front door that could've been a closet, sitting in the windowbox, drinking wine out of superhero glasses.

"Wait a second, you caught him downstairs with that woman —"

"Girl, she was a girl. She might've been sixteen."

"You caught him in the basement with this girl and threw a bunch of darts at him?"

"I didn't throw a bunch. I threw them one at a time."

"Jesus Christ, did any of them stick?"

"Not really. It was more to scare him, like in those westerns where the one guy aims his gun at the other guy's feet and says, dance, sucker."

"What did he do?"

"Kept backing up till he couldn't go any further. Moved out the next day. He waited until I left to look at cars. Came in and took everything, the dishes, the kitchen table, the bed."

"Was any of it yours?"

I nodded.

"Most of it?"

I nodded again.

"Why didn't you call the police?"

"Wasn't worth it." I dragged on my cigarette.

"Don't you want your stuff back?"

"It doesn't matter. The only thing I ever wanted him to do was talk Dave Herron into letting me into his class."

"And Daniel didn't do it?"

"Hell, no. That would be completely contrary to him. Does restore my faith in people — even when they're shits, they can stay in character." I sipped some wine. I'd known about Daniel for a long time, though I'd never said anything out loud. "There is something good that came out of all of it. If I'd taken Herron's seminar, I'd've had to drop Rhys's class."

"We never would've become friends. We are friends, right?"

"Yep." I crossed my legs. "Cady —"

"Hey, there." A black-haired woman stuck her head in. I almost fell out the window. "Didn't mean to scare you."

"Jesus Christ, Angel, would you learn to knock?" Cady managed to get her breath back before I did. "She does this at home, too," she said to me. "Try taking a shower at my house sometime."

"I'm blowing doors, hon."

"Are you going home, Angel?"

"I don't know. Do you need a ride?"

"I can walk."

"Joe Don at home?"

"I think he's spending the night with Richard again."

"Shit, ain't love grand? You want to smoke the rest of this joint?" She waved it like a miniature battle flag.

Cady grinned. So did I. "All right," Cady answered. The woman came in, slid the door shut behind her and sat on the ground by the empty wine bottle.

"Ames, this is Angel DeMartiquez. Angel, Amory."

"Nice to meet you," I said.

"That's a great name. Walker, right?"

I nodded. She lit the joint.

"I like it," she said, blowing smoke out. "Where'd you get it?"

93

"I'm guessing it came from a book, *This Side of Paradise*."

"Hell, yeah, Amory Blaine, all that shit."

Cady took a hit and handed the joint to me. It'd been a very long time and this was very good dope. I slid into it like hot water on a cold day as we passed it around.

"Your mom named you that?" Angel suddenly asked.

"I don't know. Never had the chance to ask."

Cady inhaled loud like she had emphysema or something.

"How about your dad?"

I took the joint. "Never got the chance to ask him neither."

"They get killed in a car wreck or something?"

"Jesus, Angel," Cady broke in.

"I was just wondering. You probably asked her already, anyway. That thing's almost out, give it here."

Angel took the roach from my fuzzed-out fingers and slipped it into a baggie.

"I think I'm going to roll on, unless you two want to do some more recreational law breaking."

Cady glanced at me and I started laughing the weak laugh I get when I'm high.

"I think we're just fine," she said, the left side of her face two steps behind the right in her smile.

My head bobbed up and down. "Yeah, yep, yep, yep."

The two of them started giggling. Angel ran a hand over her lips. "Fuck, I got cottonmouth."

Cady handed her glass over, the last of the pink wine floating at the bottom like cough syrup.

Angel shook her head. "Going to get me an RC, honey. That shit'll rot your brain." She pushed her sleeves up to her elbows.

94

"Is that a real leather jacket?" I asked, serious as a heart attack as she stood up.

"Yeah, yep, yep, yep," she answered with a slow lazy smile.

"I am really high, feel like I'm going to grow wings," Cady said more at Angel than to her.

> The time has come, the Walrus said,
> To talk of many things:
> Of shoes — and ships — and sealing wax —
> Of cabbages — and kings —
> And why the sea is boiling hot —
> And whether pigs have wings.

Angel recited. She pulled on her driving gloves, leaving the snaps open at the wrists, and slid the door open. "That's not to say you're a pig or anything, Cady."

"Thanks," Cady mumbled back.

"Do you know the maids with the brooms sweeping up the beach part?" It seemed very important to hear it at the time.

She smiled a wide gash of a grin, and I swear I half-expected everything but that smile to start disappearing before my very eyes.

"Hey, Angel, who's your favorite cartoon character?" asked Cady suddenly, leaning forward to catch the answer.

"Favorite cartoon character? Don't think I have one. But I always did have a thing for the Marlboro Man."

She stepped out and slid the door shut.

"Jesus."

"Yeah," said Cady, "Kind of reminds you of Zorro, doesn't she?"

* * * * *

Soon as we were sure we could both walk, we went upstairs to find Rhys, McClure, and a few other people still there.

McClure floated over. "Welcome back. I knew you hadn't left; your jackets are still here."

"What a brilliant piece of deductive logic," Cady said under her breath.

McClure took my hand and led me into the room, Cady following close behind. "Do you want anything to drink?"

My mouth felt like I'd been chewing on a towel. "Could I have a beer?"

"I'll get you one. Cady?"

"Wine, please."

McClure went her way down the hall. We sat on the floor with everyone else leaning against pillows and each other. I looked around the room twice in case being high made men disappear from my vision.

"Cady," I whispered. "There are only women here."

Cady scanned the faces and turned back to me. "My god, Amory, you're right. Not one person here with a wanger. We better end the party."

She stared hard.

I stared back.

"Does it bother you?"

"Bother me? No, I don't think so."

"Does it bother you that they're all lesbians?" She watched again as if to read my mind.

"Is it supposed to?"

"That wasn't the question."

"Being around lesbians doesn't bother me."

"Really? You don't feel threatened?"

Two seconds ago she'd been high as a kite. Now she was acting like the Gestapo. "Should I?"

"Most straight women do."

"You sure assume a lot, don't you?"

McClure came back with a beer and a glass of wine. "Here you go," she said, sitting down on top of us.

I fell asleep around five. Later I woke up to the sound of laughter and the smell of coffee, both of which dragged me down the hall in my stocking feet to the kitchen. McClure was at the table, Rhys at the sink, and Cady was standing by the stove with a spatula in hand.

"What's going on?"

"The dead have arisen!" McClure exclaimed. "Breakfast is going on. Are you hungry?"

"I think so. Can I help?" I asked, pulling my last cigarette out of the pack I managed to crush by sleeping on it.

"Nope. Want a cup of coffee?" asked Cady.

"God, yes. Please." I tried to light up. Shit, the damn thing was broken. I snapped it in half and threw it at an ashtray. Suddenly a mug of coffee was before me, steaming. "Thank you."

A lit cigarette followed. "You're welcome." Rhys smiled.

The coffee was too hot yet. I puffed the cigarette and almost threw up. "What in the hell —"

"It's made from cloves."

"It tastes like it's made from camel shit. Here." I handed it back. "I don't think I could smoke this and live."

I cleaned the crap out of my eyes, the crunchy stuff Jessie always called sleep sand, and sipped from the mug. The coffee was hot enough and strong enough to kick me awake. "Great coffee."

"Thank you," Cady said. "Now everybody get the hell out of the kitchen."

"What?" McClure looked startled.

"Get out. This is a secret recipe."

"Who'd have a secret recipe for scrambled eggs?"

"Out, especially you, McClure, you disbeliever."

They grabbed their cups and left through the dining room.

"Sure you don't want any help?"

"Can you cook?"

"I got a D in Home Ec."

Her eyebrows twitched up and down. She was so pretty there in the warm kitchen with the sun trying to find its way into the windows.

"Go on," she went on gently. "It won't take me that long."

I walked down the hall. The front room was filled with light since McClure pulled up the shades, making the wood floor seem full of sun.

"It's clean," I said, realizing the bottles were gone and the ashtrays empty.

"I picked up a little," Rhys spoke from the couch. "You sure are cute when you're asleep."

"Drooling all over my face, sure I am." I sat on the floor with my cup of coffee, the morning sun feeling good. Jess used to believe there was a heaven, used to believe she was going. Maybe her heaven was like this.

"What are you thinking about?" A voice filled my ear with the question.

"Back at my Aunt Jessie's, she had a wood floor, too. This place is nothing like her house but for that. And sometimes she'd come home from work and set down on the couch, before it was summer and got too hot, and I'd sit on the floor and we'd talk and sometimes we wouldn't.

She'd put her feet up on the coffee table and her hose would be all bunched up around her toes, you know? When I was little, she once told me angels brought me to her on a solid gold sunray and for a long time I was sure any minute a baby was going to come sliding through the window on the light of the sun. Later, though, Jess and me, her in a dress crawling up over her knees a little and me in a rock and roll T-shirt, we'd just watch the sun come in the windows, falling like honey and not expect anything else. Of course, the sun would be setting, not rising then, and I wouldn't've thought about it except for the way the room is this morning."

I turned to Cady who'd asked me in the first place. Her hair gleamed with red and gold and black all at the same time.

"Was it always like that, Ames?" McClure's voice was full as the light.

I shook my head. "A man I knew, he started digging in his garden down behind his house, in one place the dirt fell away into nothingness. He tossed a stone in after it and said he couldn't hear it land. The dirt was caving in, silent and quick like a black hole that was even pulling in all the sound. Turns out it's an old coal mine — tunnels go everywhere in the hills and under town because of the wildcatters and the crazies. I'm telling you, it does indeed make you look at solid ground twice."

* * * * *

"You won't believe what I found." Cady laughed and dragged me out of the Center, jumping around like a kid who'd just won a prize for best Halloween costume.

The air outside was thick with the smell of cut grass and sunshine. People were sitting on the lawn and the

99

sidewalks, letting the light and the heat cook winter out of their skins. I could hear mowers chopping away and a huge sprinkler fired water onto grass for the first time that spring.

"Where are we going?" I finally asked as she pulled me by the arm up an alley, a good two blocks from campus.

"A garage sale. I found the most perfect thing."

We got to the sale and she led me to a small table covered with cheap kitchen junk, pointing at a black dusty thing in one corner.

"There it is," she said proudly.

I stepped around the table trying to figure out what the hell it was. "Jesus Christ." I was looking at the biggest mother of a typewriter I'd ever seen. "Does it work?"

"I think so." She poked at the keys.

"How old do you think it is?" L.C. Smith & Corona it said in gold across the keyboard.

"I don't know. You better try it out, make sure it fits."

"Very funny." I hit the space bar a few times. It clunked and clicked each time it moved, but it did move. "Got a piece of paper?"

Cady ran off to find one.

I turned the roller, hit the keys and pressed the tab. At least the bell worked.

Cady handed me a piece of blue-lined notebook paper. I put it in and tried every letter along the rows then typed Amory Amory Amory.

"Let me try," she said. Cady Cady Cady, she typed, and I am Beautiful.

"You sure are," I said under my breath.

"You like it?"

I nodded. My nose was starting to itch way inside, probably from all the dust and old fertilizer in the garage. Ten dollars was scrawled on a piece of masking tape stuck to the top. I looked over at the woman having the sale. "I'll give you six bucks for this here thing, this typewriter. It kind of sticks and needs a new ribbon."

She left her money box and her coffee cup in the care of the radio and trotted across the garage to us. "I'll let it go for eight."

"Sold."

The garage sale lady smiled as she took my money. "Need anything else? Got some chairs and a hair dryer and some nice clothes for sale, all in good shape."

"No thanks," Cady shouted back, then lowered her voice. "I was thinking of buying that Schwinn bicycle, but if I rode it around everybody'd start calling me Alice B. Toeclips."

I couldn't say a word. Picking up the typewriter I found the damn thing weighed near to thirty pounds. Stopping every half block to let arms and hands get unnumbed, we managed to get it to my room.

"Looks pretty good there," Cady said when I finally cleared enough shit off the desk to set it down.

"It sure do."

"Guess this means you're all set."

"Yeah, I suppose it does. It does indeed." I hit the space bar again, making the typewriter thump the desk. I didn't know if I was going to write anything worth reading on this damn thing but it sure was going to keep the girl next door awake. She hates noise, even if I don't think I'm being too loud. Before, if I wanted to type anything I got stuck sitting down in the study next to the laundry room where the school typewriters are bike-chained to old, old desks. It's creepy down there, especially late at night and the pipes rattle and hum and do other shit that pipes do.

I didn't have to worry at all about the girl in the room next door and the typewriter looked even better on the desk McClure and I made out of bricks and boards after I moved in with her later that week. She invited me to live with her and I said okay. She conned Rhys into letting us use her car, so we moved on Friday, bought a futon for me Saturday and went stealing from construction sites on Sunday. McClure was real good at swiping stuff without making a sound or stepping on nails or anything.

I got the bedroom upstairs with sloping ceilings. It smelled like dryers in the summer when I first moved in, so I burned some incense, which didn't help, and forced open the windows, which did.

* * * * *

Get up. Stumble to the desk. Light a cigarette. Turn on the reading lamp. Pull the T-shirt as far down as it will go so when I sit down, the cold seat of the chair isn't as much of a shock. The letters on the white keys seem splintered, hairlined instead of solid black. Probably because they are, this damn machine is so old.

McClure says this'll help get me going. Build up a portfolio, she says. For what, I want to ask. It all seems so full of nothing. But it gives me a job and I've got a place to live. And yesterday I found my first gray hair, so I guess that means I'm growing up.

Sometimes, most times, I feel like a piece of dust ticking out of the woodwork and into the sun, looking for a place to land but then a breeze from someone rushing by shoves me into circles all over again.

Three fucking pages take too fucking long at four o'clock in the morning.

* * * * *

School ended and summer came, each day oozing into weeks then months with me working at Juniper's, sorting books, dusting shelves, and catching shoplifters. I missed Cady; I hadn't seen her since I moved and then she went off to New York or New Hampshire to work. I wrote letters to her all the time, even kept a notebook by my bed. There was so much I wanted to tell her that I was afraid if I tore out a sheet of paper I'd forget something important, so I never sent them. McClure took off to see her big brother for a while, leaving me alone. Strange weather started September. I woke up on two different nights to put on a sweatshirt because I was freezing.

I got to the door just as the bell rang for the third time. "All right, goddammit." I yanked the door open.

"Nice outfit," Cady Baird said, nodding at my towel. She stepped past me into the house and walked up the stairs. I followed, the trail of water on the floor from the bathroom already cold under my feet.

She had the coffee out and was dumping teaspoons into the coffeemaker. "Where's McClure?"

"Brother's. Rhys is at a conference."

"International Feminist Book thing. Aren't you cold?"

I looked down at my legs. My toenails were beginning to turn blue.

"Go put some clothes on. I'll wait."

For a second she looked like a red-haired she-wolf, I swear to god. Still chilled, I came back to find the coffee poured and Cady at the table.

103

"You cut your hair."

"Yours is longer," she said back.

"I decided to let it do what it wanted." I sipped my coffee.

"Have any cigarettes?"

I shook my head.

Her eyebrow went up. "You quit?"

"Sort of. You started?"

"Sort of." She gave me the kind of smile she'd give someone passing her on the street.

"So what's up your ass?"

She twisted the gold band she wears on her wedding ring finger. "I was —" She stopped. Her hands fell to her lap. "I don't know."

It got quiet except for the funny sounds of the coffeemaker; she'd made a full pot.

"Amory?"

I looked up from my cup. Grease rainbows that float on top are universal.

"As long as I've known you, I've never cooked you dinner. Would you like to come over tonight?"

"Tonight?"

She nodded, then smiled her usual smile that seemed to light up her side of the kitchen.

"What time?"

"Eight. Think you can be ready by then?"

"Hell, I already took a shower."

* * * * *

"Hi," she said from the screened porch of her house on Dooley Street.

"Evening," I answered. The size of the house knocked the shit out of me. I gawked around. "How did you get this place?"

"Joe Don found it three months ago. The lady who owns it is ninety years old and lives in a retirement community in Florida."

"You lucked out." I meant it. The living room was long and wide with a staircase that rose up along the wall to curve at the top. The furniture was heavy and big, in too good shape to be theirs. "Whose sofa and stuff?"

"Mrs. Hortenberry's. She left just about everything for us."

"That was nice of her."

"She's a nice lady, a little strange about the house, but nice. She sends us postcards, but they're not really to us. I think she wants us to read them aloud in every room so the house doesn't get too lonely and fall off its foundation."

I pulled off my sweatshirt and threw it on a chair. "Angel doesn't live with you anymore?"

"She has the attic." Cady pointed at the ceiling. "All the light and room she could possibly hope for. Would you like a beer?"

"Sure. Where is she?"

"Took off for a couple of weeks." Cady walked through the dining room. "She does that every now and then." She disappeared through an archway and into the kitchen, only to be back in a second with two bottles. "She wants to do a painting of you."

That was a jolt. "What?"

"She wants to do a painting." Cady sipped. "A nude. I think it will be stunning by the way she was talking about it."

"No."

"Angel's not like McClure. She never talks about her work, so she must be really excited —"

I cut her off with a look.

"What's the matter, afraid she'd leap on you soon as you drop your pants?"

"What in the hell is that supposed to mean?"

She walked toward the kitchen. "As lovely as you are, Amory Walker, not even you could make Angel DeMartiquez swing."

"Thanks. You do wonders for a woman's ego." I drank some beer.

"Oh, don't get me wrong," she said, hanging around the arch. "That isn't to say you aren't tempting to some of us."

Up till that second I'd been hungry. Now what felt like a small kitten began doing yoga stretches in the middle of my stomach. I took a deep breath and stared at a portrait on a stereo speaker; Cady and her family in front of a fireplace. She's not smiling but her little brother is, and in the school picture stuck in the corner of the frame, he's got a big grin. I never knew autistic kids smiled, thought they just sat in the corner humming to themselves.

I paced slowly, looking at the murals painted on the walls. Recent additions, telling by the jars of paint and the brushes drying to stiffness on top of one of those tables that always look like they should be holding a cremation vase or a fake marble statue of some guy with no eyes. A stallion in blues filled floor to ceiling near the front door; to the left, strips of wall around the high windows were filled with scraps of graffiti in a hundred colors. On the third wall across from the windows was a sketch in red, rough and delicate all at the same time, of two naked women holding one another. I stepped closer. The sun

106

stretched through the panes of glass and stroked them gold from shoulder to thigh, touching the way they would touch one another.

"Amory?"

I turned. The same color gleamed in Cady's hair and eyes, streaking fire and light. What would it be like to be that close to her?

"Dinner's ready."

I carried my beer to the dining room table. Fuck, maybe I should leave, the table was set with different forks and everything. Cady came in with a bottle and a corkscrew.

"Open this while I get the food?"

I nodded yes as her hand brushed mine.

Bits of cork gathered on the bottom of the glasses, magnified by the wine and looking like broken bits of dog food. The candles were lit. I stood behind a chair, not sure who had the right of way as far as feminist social graces go. "Why are we standing here like idiots while the food is getting cold?"

"I don't know, Amory, honey, but that's a very good question." She laughed and we both sat down.

A thin silver necklace hung at her throat, the gleam of candlelight turning it almost white. I watched as she spoke, the light slipping one way then the other with every movement.

"So I came back to get my degree. Now I'm thinking about graduate school. Why? Why did you come to Chase, really?" She laid her napkin beside her empty plate.

"Maybe it had something to do with having nowhere else to go," I answered.

Cady grinned. "Well, I have somewhere else to go. To the can." She stood up. "What do you say we move this party into the other room? I think there's another bottle in the refrigerator and I have a new tape of Jill's you should hear."

I went on a search for the wine. It was on the bottom shelf lying on its side next to the carrots. I opened the bottle and took it and the glasses into the other room, stopping only for the candlestick holder still on the table. The two candles were burned halfway, the melted wax looking like soft tree bark. A door opened far away and I stood waiting by the coffee table for her to come back.

"Great," Cady said, walking in.

I handed her a glass. "This one's yours."

"You're sure?"

"I took special care. Wouldn't want you to get girl germs."

She nodded and held it up. "Skoal."

"Here's mud in your eye."

Our glasses chimed and we both drank, her looking at me and me trying to look at anything but her. It got very quiet.

"What about that tape?" I asked.

"I'll put it on. You sit down."

Soon music slipped out of the speakers and into the room.

"She is really good," Cady said after two songs. She was holding herself tight and strong with her knees pulled up and her chin on her arm, curled up in a white shirt and no-longer-blue jeans and her bare feet tucked neatly together. The music began again, slipping across her rounded back and shoulders and into shadows and colors of the room till the tape rolled to an end.

"Why didn't you write?" Cady asked softly.

Shit. "I did."

"I never got your letters."

"I never sent them."

"Why not?"

"They aren't finished. They're in a notebook by my bed. That's when I wrote you, when I was in bed."

"Alone, I hope." She grinned.

I smiled at the wine glass in my hands. "Yes."

"I thought —" She bit her lip, "that maybe you got scared."

Silence grew as thick as the dark away from the candlelight. What should I do now? Leave? Propose? Suggest a nice quiet game of gin rummy?

"I think you're beautiful," she said simply.

My stomach fell on the floor. Before I had time to pick it up, she set her wine glass on the table and slid toward me. She took my hand, a hand that felt numb till the second she kissed my fingers one by one, her mouth touching like a dance. The gold and shadow edged across her face, and I reached around her neck to touch her hair, expecting a burn, knowing I'd been wanting to do this since the first time I saw her.

Barely a touch this kiss, like mouths whispering together. Her hands came to my face, pulling me closer till tongues curled and electric sparks flashed behind my eyes. I twined and twisted her hair, practically feeling the blazing red that was soft and wild and warm. She leaned away, the kiss smoothing into air.

Her eyes seemed so deep I could fall into them. She traced the edges of my lips and the curves of my cheekbones, touching like my face was a raised map and she a blind woman trying to find the shape of the land. I squeezed my eyes shut again as she brushed my neck with the tips of her fingers, throwing sparks that seemed to grow and pinwheel into my head from where they'd begun, leaving me half-frozen with the hot and cold of it.

I felt the shapes of her fingers on my eyelids, then on the crescent scar. She touched the small overlap of skin that followed the exact curve of bone beneath. Opening my eyes, I watched Cady grow serious and gentle, asking what she would never say with words again.

"It was," I began, reaching for my wine glass, "a long time ago."

I took a sip and returned the glass to the table, trying to match the rim with the small damp circle left there. A flick of my finger, the glass rang a single note and the wine made waves that bounced to the sides and back that got confused whether they were coming or going.

"I was fifteen, but I wanted to be sixteen so I told everybody I almost was. I was walking home from school down Memorial Boulevard reading a book or something."

I tapped it again, and the glass rang out.

"It was spring, beautiful outside, the snow finally gone and everything turning green, though it was still too cold to go barefoot. I knew because I'd left my shoes on the front steps the day before to walk around the yard and the ground was cold and slick under my feet. I was always running around barefoot when I was a little kid, drove Jessie batshit."

I drank some more, the glass a hard, unbreakable shell in my hand making me think of that trick where somebody tries to crack an egg by squeezing it in her fist.

"He stepped out of nowhere, and I mean nowhere since it was a good ten feet from the road to where the woods started. Jackie was his name, Jackie Macon, and I don't know where he'd been hiding but he was all of a sudden standing there in front of me. Come here, he said, I got to show you something."

I noticed when the candlelight fell into the wine, it came out on the table in two wings.

110

"Never liked Jackie. He was always sort of creepy. Once he crucified a cat and left it hanging on two-by-fours in the playground. No one did anything, of course, since he was a Macon and they own practically the whole fucking town, Macon Township, Macon Mines. Even the road we lived on was Macon Memorial Boulevard and it ran all the way around Sterling and out to the country like a dog collar and a leash."

I moved the glass around, trying to make the wings of light come together but they never did, just the places where the light fell heaviest, the two bright ovals that looked like where the wings should be attached.

"But there he was. Come here, got to show you something, he says. He's a big guy, and he had long black hair that was always swinging in his face and he had me by the arm and half dragged me into the woods. I was trying to find out which direction we were going since he was going so fast and kept jumping around, and then he stopped. He just stopped dragging me. Simplicity, he said, want simplicity."

I knotted my hands as if playing here's the church and here's the steeple, so hard my knuckles went white and my fingers went red.

"So I said, what, what do you want, trying to figure a way to get the hell out of there when he pulls this knife. Simplicity, I want simplicity, he kept saying while I was trying to figure out what the fuck that meant and trying to stay away from the knife. God, it looked so big to me, being on the blade end of it. It couldn't have been more than a pocket knife but it was huge, seemed as long as his whole hand. We were in this clearing, so far into the woods I wasn't sure where the road was. And he stopped talking, stopped walking, just stood there with that knife. And he let go of me. Gripped my arm so tight it hurt more when he let loose his hand than when he'd been hanging on."

I pulled my hands apart, reaching to touch the scar on my face.

"He hit me. With the butt of the knife in his fist. Must have had another blade on the end because I started bleeding so much I couldn't see out this eye. He kept swinging and I fell and he didn't stop, he just went on hitting me. And when he thought I couldn't move anymore, he tore what he could of my jeans and cut the rest away with his knife, and ripped my shirt open. I got scratches from his fingernails that stretched all the way across and turned into welts later."

My throat burned with the talk. I drank more of the wine, the wings of light blurring then getting lost in the dark.

"And he raped me there in that field and I swear to god it was like I was standing over him watching while he did this to me. Got to feeling like I was moving all over the field, seeing from a thousand different ways and not feeling any of it. Till I opened my eyes and his shirt was red and his hands were red and I'd thought he was all done with it, all done, and I hurt so bad I couldn't feel anything but the weeds crisscrossing against my back."

I set the glass on the table, pushing the rim into my palm.

"Then he took that knife, he took it and put it between my legs then inside and it burned like he'd poured a line of gasoline and lit a match to my skin. I couldn't scream, couldn't even move."

The rim of my glass spun the candlelight almost into a perfect circle.

"Jackie looked at me, he looked at me and smiled and said now my mark's on you, and leaned down to kiss my mouth. Then he left. Left me there thinking I was going to die from what he done."

I ran my fingers down the stem of the glass, feeling how perfect the cut edges were.

"I woke up in a hospital, in a room all white and gray since they pulled the curtains shut so I could sleep and I thought they'd put a sheet over my head because I was dead."

I drank the last of my wine, the bits of cork leaving a trail on the side.

"I got this other scar, too." I unbuttoned my jeans, pointing at the top. Even in the soft light it was pinkish and stretched, curving up and looking only half-healed though the last stitches had come out six years ago. "Simplicity. I figured that out. He was saying some pussy. He wanted some pussy."

There in the candlelight Cady watched me, tears slipping from her eyes.

"I never called it rape before."

She didn't hide her face, didn't wipe away her crying.

"I never talked about it to anybody, even when they sent social workers to try and make me. I never thought it was any of their business."

"And me?" she asked quietly. "Is it mine?"

"No." I shook my head. Is it? "But I wanted to tell you anyway."

She bent over, and slowly buttoned my pants back up. Her arms went around my shoulders, laying my head against her breasts, and she rocked me back and forth while the candles burned.

portrait

"What in the hell?" I was standing behind Joe Don outside the bathroom.

"Dammit, J.D., where is my shampoo?" Cady yelled again.

"You don't have to scream anymore, I can hear. And you woke up your guest."

"I was already awake," I mumbled. As soon as Cady had stood up naked from her futon I decided to get dressed. The yelling started just as I was putting on my socks.

"Did you take my shampoo?"

"I wouldn't think of washing my hair with coupon-special shampoo."

"Cut the shit, buddy. You know exactly which shampoo is mine."

"So that was yours. It's rather expensive, don't you think? Very p.i."

"I know how much it costs, J.D., I bought it, remember? Now where is it?" Her voice was threatening. I don't know how anybody else would've reacted, but Joe Don was drawing on the steamed-up mirror and not paying her any attention. Her face disappeared and the water went off. The shower curtain slid open, folding up on itself, and she stepped, wet and naked, out of the bathtub.

"I'm going to kill you, Joey," she said.

I peeked around him. Her nipples were pink and hardening in the cold air.

"Now get hold of yourself, Cady," he said, hands up and backing away from the crazy naked woman. "Oh, Amory," he said, pleased he had someone to hide behind, "I thought it was you. How are you doing?" he asked, stepping around me.

Cady kept getting closer. "I'm going to throw you in your vegamatic and turn it on fricassee."

"Don't let this little scene bother you," he continued with an elbow on my shoulder. "She's very violent for a pacificist."

Armed with a tube of toothpaste, she waved it around like she meant business. "If you don't get my shampoo, I am going to show you how to prevent tooth decay all over your body."

"But I like my body cavities. Be careful, darling. Walking around bare-assed can be harmful to your health, not to mention your reputation. Besides, you might drive me mad with desire."

Close enough so I could see drops of water sliding down her skin, she turned her head to look at me. "Hi," I said, watching one single stream gliding down her cheek to her lip.

"Hi," she said back, her eyes filling mine. Her face was square and strong, the corded muscles in her neck emptying a small, hollow place at the base of her throat. The necklace she'd been wearing, the one I'd twirled around and around my finger as she slept, wasn't there anymore.

"What a touching scene," Joe Don chimed, now at the end of the hall and out of danger. "Would look lovely in a movie."

She snapped back, ready to deal with the boy wonder. I flattened myself against the wall so's to let her by.

"Get my shampoo, Joe Don."

"Oh, all right." He crossed his arms. "On one condition."

She tilted her head, listening.

"Don't come home until after midnight."

"Can't you and Richard fuck and suck in the afternoons?"

"A candlelight dinner isn't romantic while the sun is still shining, Cady. And really, your language."

"All right," she said, putting her hands on her hips. "All right. You've got a deal. Hurry up, I'm getting cold."

Joe Don dashed away to get the ripped-off shampoo.

Cady turned around, letting me see every square, bare, and glorious inch of her. She was curved and pale like the lady on the seashell rising out of the ocean. The hair under her arms and on her legs was red and so was the triangle of curls between her hips. I suddenly felt like a pair of hands had found a way to the inside of my thighs and were now kneading their way out.

She leaned over and kissed me, then walked back to finish her shower.

119

The coffee was done when she walked into the kitchen, rubbing her wet hair with a royal blue towel. We sat at the table and talked and laughed. Last night lay on the table between us. She'd taken me to bed and held me till I fell asleep, naked and warm and no bad dreams.

Joe Don had left when the light against the windows was the silver of morning and when he came back with a bag of groceries and a shoe box, it was warm afternoon gold against the window panes. He pretended to be upset that we'd been wasting our time smoking and talking; the least we could've done was change his sheets, he said.

"What's in the box, Joe Don?" Cady asked, poking around.

"Do you want to see? They're brand new shoes. I just got them." He finished putting the groceries away and came over with a steak knife to cut the string wrapped around on both sides. The box top fell on the floor along with the tissue in his hurry to pull out a pair of gold, spike-heeled fancy sandals.

"Wow," she said.

"Yeah." I'd seen shoes like that before, but never that big. "Where did you get them?"

"There's a terrific store that carries every kind of shoe you can imagine. We can go sometime if you'd like." He kicked off a loafer and shoved his foot into the right sandal. "What do you think?" asked J.D., holding up his pant leg for us to get a better look.

"They're okay," I said, not knowing what else to say.

"I can't really tell. Put on the other one."

Joe Don strapped on the left one and twirled in front of us. "I love them. And they're so comfortable."

I sort of nodded. I wouldn't be caught dead in a pair of shoes like that. In fact, I'd have to be dead for anybody to ever get them on me. "What size are they?"

120

"Fourteen."

"You know," Cady began, "I think I like them. Spin around again, Joey."

He spun and stepped around the kitchen, twitching his cute little butt. He knew how to walk in them better than most of the girls I know.

"Yes," she nodded, "I like them."

"Amory doesn't," Joe Don said, looking at me.

"I didn't say that." My face got hot.

"Well, it doesn't matter. I just hope Richard does." Sighing, he sat on the kitchen floor to take them off. "I usually don't buy such flashy shoes since my feet are so big, but I thought I'd surprise him." He put the shoes carefully inside themselves, toe in heel, and back in the box. Joe Don looked up at me and gave me a big smile. I smiled back. My God, he was good-looking, blonde and tan with deep blue eyes. People like that should never have to worry about pleasing anybody; they could sit in the middle of a kitchen floor like J.D. was doing and let everybody look at them. "I understand if it bothers you, Amory. Sometimes it bothers me."

"What does?"

"Dressing in drag. But if Richard likes it, then I don't mind."

"It's not that it bothers me, Joe Don, if it's what you want. I just don't understand it."

He stood up. "We all have our little weirdnesses."

"But why ask for trouble when gay guys got more than enough these days?"

"Honey —" Joe Don picked up my cigarette pack, asking to have one. I nodded yes. "There's such a thing as a faggot fire drill. Do you know what that is?"

"No."

121

"Well —" He lit a match, "it's when all the gays run out of a burning building —" He lit the cigarette, waving the match to put it out, "and at the first opportunity they turn around and run back in." With a precise toss, the dead match spun from his long, thin fingers to the ashtray. He smiled again. "And you wondered why I lettered in basketball."

I blew a smoke ring. Faggot fire drill.

Joe Don suddenly sat down at the table, leaning in close like we were all going to start talking drug deals. "Amory, it's just one of those things you have to accept about the human condition. For instance, I saw the most gorgeous man at the supermarket. Wonderful to look at, and I was about to walk over and introduce myself, suggest a nice quiet evening of fucking then propose marriage, when this young woman sauntered over and kissed him on the mouth."

"Oh, no," I said.

"Oh, gross," said Cady.

"Oh, yes," he went on. "Just another weirdness that infects the population, the breeder mentality. Always doing things like that to show what they are, like kissing on the sidewalk or having babies. Ramming it down people's throats, so to speak." He giggled and glanced at his gold wristwatch. "Care for a condom before you go?"

Cady grinned. "We better leave. If we don't, he'll do something disgusting. Last time he started blowing up his rubbers like balloons."

I checked my pack of cigarettes; between the three of us, we'd managed to finish over half of them already. Christ.

"He doesn't see many people anymore," she said, as we walked towards town to get her french fries and me cigarettes. I was going to have to buy two packs this time.

122

"Joe Don?"

"Yeah. He's a great guy and people used to have him over all the time for dinner or parties, even if they didn't know him. He's so funny and smart —"

"— and good-looking —"

"That, too, but nobody calls him up and nobody drops over anymore."

"Why not? Without him the basketball team would be shit."

"I don't know. His politics, AIDS, their stupidity. He's always been out, back in prep school he told everyone he was gay. They still liked him. Now all he has is Richard."

"He has you and Angel."

"It's not the same. Seems ever since we started making an issue of gay and lesbian rights, he's gotten the axe and I've gotten hero status. He hardly goes out."

"Take him with you."

"He doesn't like dyke parties. I don't blame him. At first he told me it was because there was no one to flirt with. Then he said that lesbians take themselves way too seriously. Then he cried a little bit and said that we scare him. Imagine that. Said we treated him like he wasn't even there and now even his straight friends are doing it."

We walked down the sidewalk, our steps matching.

"If lesbians scare him, why does he live with you?"

"I met J.D. when I was a gay woman, not when I was a lesbian."

"There's a difference?"

"It's the difference between living a lie and living the truth. Gay women uphold the myths of dykedom; lesbians are trying to tear those myths apart."

"And you're a lesbian now?"

"The real question —" She smiled and looped her arm through mine, "is which one are you?"

123

*****

A party for my birthday. McClure dreamed it up and announced it to Cady and me as we walked in the door.

"Don't you want a party?"

"What kind of party?"

"A good party. All the fun people will be here; the duds can stay at home."

"Okay," I shrugged. "But I barely know enough people to fill the front closet. And most of you won't go to a party if it meant going back in there."

Cady giggled.

"When?"

"Tomorrow. Is that enough time for you?"

"She's been planning this for three weeks, Ames," Cady stuck in.

"Huh?"

"It was going to be a surprise party but I thought maybe you'd want to know about it." McClure handed me a piece of paper. "Here's the list."

All her friends, not a bad one in the bunch. I smiled.

"Is there anyone else you'd like to invite?"

"Joe Don Barrett. And he can bring a guest."

"Okay."

"Is there anything I can do to help?"

"Why don't you get some more junk food? I have some, but we'll need some more."

"Pretzels, that kind of stuff? All right. What time does this wingding start?"

"Nine o'clock," Cady answered.

"Terrific," I said. "Terrific."

The black sports car skidded to a stop, sounding like a cat that'd been stepped on, then backed down the street. The tinted window on the passenger side slid down.

"Hey, Amory, you want a ride?"

I walked closer, trying to figure out who the fuck was behind the black reflector sunglasses.

"Come on, jump in," she said, putting the car into gear.

"How you doing, Angel?" I slammed the car door shut.

"All right," she answered, flashing her perfect teeth in a smile, then looking back down the street. The car fishtailed and we managed to cover half the block going sideways. "Where you headed?"

"Grocery store." I'd meant to get up early, but didn't.

"Picking up stuff for the party tonight?"

"Yeah." I watched the leaves in the street skate out of the way as the Triumph roared up. Angel drove like a fucking maniac.

"I really like your name."

She surprised me. "What?"

"I do, for real. I like McClure's name, too, but she gave that to herself. That was her mom's name before she got married." The car swerved around an Oldsmobile that was going the speed limit. "I hate people who drive slow. It's better than being named after somebody in *War and Peace*."

"I haven't read it."

"Nobody has. They all memorized the Classic Comic."

"You can call me Ames, if you want." I leaned to the right, hoping my weight would help the car take the curve.

"I'll stick with Amory. It's sexy, just like the woman."

I swallowed hard. Cady said Angel was straight as an arrow.

Her gloved fingers drummed the wheel as we waited for the green light. "Fuck, I hate being stopped. So what do you do with yourself, Amory Walker?"

"Write. I'm a writer."

"You like sleeping with my roommate?"

It got a little frosty on the inside of the car.

"Okay, okay, it was a joke," she said, looking from the road to me and back again. "What's your major?"

"Angel, if you can't come up with anything better than that, drop me off at the next bus stop."

Her leather jacket creaked when she twitched her shoulders. "I can't ask you what your sign is because today is your birthday and that would make you a Libra. I can't ask if you come here often because it's my car and I've never given you a ride. The first question was none of my business, the second is out and out stupid, but I'm sort of up a creek without a television set, see?"

"I reckon."

"Now anything worth asking you will have to be done over drinks. You want to get a beer?"

"Sure." She was really cute, even though the shades weirded me out. They reminded me of the x-ray glasses advertised in comic books; she could see through everybody but nobody could see in.

Angel pulled into a parking lot. The only thing around besides ourselves was a Volkswagen bug that looked like it'd been nuked, and a square building with a neon bar and grill sign that faded to nothing next to the afternoon sun.

"Never been here before, have you?"

"Haven't had the pleasure."

She opened the door to the bar. Angelo's, it said below the small window. "Its a real dive but it bops on the weekends. See over there?" She pointed to a dark corner as I shrugged off my jean jacket. Be too cold to wear it pretty soon. "Musicians come down to play. Sometimes they're the cream of the litter box and people throw beer bottles at them."

"And if you're good they just throw the beer?"

"If you're any good you get a rep and a time slot to play for money." She tossed her sunglasses onto a table. "Sit down."

A short man with a hooked nose set a shot in front of her, then looked at me with his hands folded.

"You just want a beer, right?" Angel shoved her sleeves further up her arms.

I nodded. The man came back with a mug of beer.

"Gracias, Angelo, thanks." Knocking back the clear liquid now that I had something to drink, too, she set the empty shot glass upside down on the table. Angelo returned with two more.

"What kind of stuff do you write?"

"Everything." My beer was full enough to send little streams down the sides every time one of us touched the table. I slurped at the top. "That's dull. Let's talk about you instead."

"One of my favorite subjects," she said, drinking half of one of the glasses.

"What do you do?"

"I go to graduate school."

"That's all?"

"I'm a painter."

"What kind of painting?"

"Right now I'm doing portraits. How people look to me. I work with other stuff as well."

"But mostly paints?"

"Yes. The colors are all mine."

"Are you any good?"

"Good enough to paint you," Angel answered, finishing the glass and setting it next to the first, a matching crystal set.

Shit. I swallowed my beer like Kool-Aid. "Thanks, but no thanks, Angel."

"Good enough to get invited to Florence."

"Why don't you go?"

"I did. I was there for three months. Then I was, how shall we say, uninvited." The third shot was gone and the last glass turned over. "You should really drink this instead of that crap, Amory. Tequila. The good stuff. He has a special friend who gets it from Mexico. Thanks, Angelo," she finished as he set two more in front of her and a shot and a beer in front of me.

"He sure is quiet," I said soon as he left.

"Got his tongue cut out in Ecuador."

"What for?"

"Smuggling."

"Why aren't you in Florence, if you don't mind me asking."

"Amory, you can ask me any damn thing you want." She ran her finger around the rim of the nearest glass. "That doesn't necessarily mean I'll answer. You like my murals?"

"Yes," I answered truthfully. I swallowed the shot and chased it with beer. The tequila was slick as ice.

"Good stuff, huh?"

"Yeah. Smooth." I think she was talking about the tequila.

"You should come up to my studio some time."

"Hate to tell you, Angel, but that's a very old line."

She grinned over her glass. "Amory, you are one of the most striking women I have ever seen. No, you are one of the most striking human beings I've ever seen. Ice-blue eyes and those cheekbones sharp enough to give paper cuts. But as much as I like the way you look, you just aren't my type, doll."

I grinned back. "And who is your type?"

"It ain't exactly who as much as what. Hell, I can make beautiful music with anybody, but not without a baton." Angel laughed hard enough to make the table shake and the tequila spill over. She quieted down, slammed the last shot and stood up. "Angelo," she shouted across the bar, "Angelo, put it on my tab, man, gracias, aloha." She put on her sunglasses and headed for the door.

"I owe you, Angel."

"Don't worry about it. I pay at the end of the month. He charges me bulk rate."

Angel didn't feel like answering any more questions, even when I asked where the hell we were going. She stopped at a grocery store. I got what I needed and we raced out of the parking lot, she gunning the engine to scare the little old ladies pushing grocery carts and me near to death. I love cars and I don't mind crazy-ass drivers, but I sure would've felt a lot better if she'd at least made a move towards the brakes at the stop signs.

"Damn keys," I muttered as the door swung open. The tequila was making little noises in my head by the time we got back to the apartment. "Hi, McClure."

"I heard you clomping all the way up the stairs in those boots. Who dropped you off? The tires squealed all the way down the street. Sounded like Angel DeMartiquez."

"It was Angel DeMartiquez. Here, I got you all kinds of shit for tonight." I handed her the bags I managed to fill with almost every kind of potato chip and pretzel in the store while running down the aisles.

"You got a ride from Angel? You smell like beer."

"I've been drinking it."

"Amory." She gave me a thorough up and down. "Are you smashed?"

"Smashed? Of course not. I never get smashed." I flopped onto the couch and watched the ceiling. "Oh, no, there are bugs coming out of the walls!" I flung my arms over my head, pretending to be Ray Milland in *The Lost Weekend*.

"You should quit writing and go into acting," she said, setting the bags on the coffee table.

"Cady did that, but backasswards." I always felt sorry for Ray Milland, especially when he was wandering the streets looking for somehere to hock his typewriter.

"What?"

"Cady was an actor then she got into politics."

"You are drunk. You're not making any sense." She leaned against the couch and peered down at me. I could see her between my arms.

"I am, too." I sat up. "I'm making perfect sense. You're just not listening. What's wrong?"

"What makes you think anything is wrong?"

"Come on, you can tell me."

"I don't want to talk about it."

"Okay."

She stepped around the end of the couch and sat down. Maybe we needed to re-arrange the furniture; I was getting tired of the way it was.

"Tell me this," I said, "if you were a newspaper, would this make the first page?"

McClure smiled sadly and shook her head.

"It has to be love."

Looking straight at me, she gave me a grin like I wasn't supposed to guess but she was glad I did anyway.

130

"Jesus. You and Cady hate to unburden your souls unless you already have the answers. Let me give you some advice —"

"Oh, god, not you, too."

"Don't interrupt, it's rude." I patted my pockets for cigarettes. "Lovers are like confetti."

"Confetti?"

"Confetti." I found the pack and pulled out a cigarette and matches. "Give them a toss and you'd think you never saw anything so pretty. But once they've hit the cold concrete floor, you don't think of them anymore, you go looking for another handful of glitter."

She thought about this for a second while I lit up. Leaning closer, she took a deep breath. "What do you think of Cady Baird?"

I blew out a lungful of smoke and considered the question. "Why? You got the hots for her?"

"No," she laughed. "I have the hots for someone else." McClure got serious and slapped her palm flat against her thigh. "Someone else, Amory."

"Cady Baird? She's beautiful and I love her," I answered, sounding like a munchkin.

"God, Ames," she laughed again.

I inhaled again, thin whiffs of incense burned days ago getting through the cigarette smoke.

"You went for a drink with Angel DeMartiquez. She must like you a lot."

"It's my celestial beauty."

"It might be," McClure said seriously. "She's a great painter. She does everything alone."

"Maybe that's why she's great."

"You've seen her stuff?"

"Some."

131

"There's a whole series she did hanging in Martin Luther King, Jr. Memorial Hall. She submitted her work under an alias and when she won, she donated the paintings."

"Why didn't she tell them who she was?"

"Students weren't supposed to compete. I don't know why she gave her work away, though I think it had something to do with her not needing the money. She disappeared right after that."

"She went to Florence. Then she got uninvited. What time does the party start?"

"Nine. I wonder what she's doing now."

"Portraits. Want to hand me the Frito's?"

"God, that was all about two years ago. You were just a freshman, Ames."

"Freshwoman."

"Okay, freshwoman."

"How about freshling? It's nonsexist and still derogatory." I leaned back to look at the ceiling again. It was smooth and shadowless. "See? I'm learning."

"I remember that gallery opening. It was packed."

"How about those Frito's, pal?"

She set the Frito's and two cans of beer on the table, laughing quiet-like, and stopped suddenly. "Amory, do you think you'll fall in love with Cady Baird?"

"McClure, if I fall in love with anybody, it'll be a fucking miracle. Open the bag, will you?"

* * * * *

"Last three weeks, seems like I've spent half my life trying to figure out who I am and the rest trying to accept it." She sighed.

132

I finished my third can of beer and looked at her. There were corn chips stuck in my teeth; if I smiled it'd be a punishment to look at me. I nodded again. We'd been sitting on the couch, the living room getting darker, letting time go by. It was a shocker when the doorbell rang.

McClure pulled out her pocket watch. "Jesus, I'll bet that's someone for the party."

"Want me to get the goddamn door?"

"You're the guest of honor. Put the groceries away instead." She got off the couch. "You better behave yourself tonight or I'll scramble your eggs."

"You forget, I don't understand ovarian humor." I was halfway down the hall with the bags by the time the door opened.

The party went along fine. People came and talked and listened to music. Eleven o'clock and Cady still hadn't shown. Joe Don showed up in pink knickers with Richard at his side and Angel high as a kite behind them. J.D. gave me a kiss on the cheek and Angel gave me a doobie thick as my finger. I'd already opened the rest of my presents, or somebody opened them for me, and everyone was having a good time. Everybody I could think of was there except her.

Where is she? I sat on the wood steps to my room. Last time I saw Cady she kissed me at the front door last night. Maybe she's changed her mind, maybe she thinks I'm playing games, maybe she isn't who I think she is, maybe she's playing games, not thinking I'm open to the idea.

What idea? What fucking idea? That she and me would be lovers now since she held me while the moon turned her room the color blue and she whispered and rocked me while I cried into her skin like a baby? It didn't

133

mean anything, it was just friendship and she didn't, couldn't think it was any more. She can't think it's anything more. Angel thought there was, but Angel didn't know and Joe Don knew it was me upstairs sleeping with Cady but he didn't know a thing either.

The grain of the wood in the door looked like an owl crying because its nest was burned down. Sort of like a smokey the bear poster.

She said she'd be here tonight. She told me before she left, when we looked at the clouds moving swift across the moon. She knew about the party before I did since it was supposed to be a surprise and all. What in the hell am I doing? Jessie was right, I am a freak. I like Cady, but not the way Cady thinks, I don't think I do, but what if it's true, I mean, what if I am gay? What if I am a lesbian? So what if I am? So big fucking deal, who's to care, anyway? Jess won't because she'd deader than a doornail and if she's spinning in her grave, there ain't no one out there to hear her anyhow. So who cares what the stumpjumpers in West Virginia think? So what if I like Cady Baird, so what if I'm happy, so what if I wish she were here and everybody else would go home so we could sneak into my room at the top of the house?

But what am I going to do? I've never been with a woman before, not like that. What if I'm no good at it? What am I supposed to do? She's not here because she saw that damn scar and it's ugly and I showed it to her. But that can't be true. She cried. In her living room, Cady cried quiet as the candlelight and held on to me as we lay under the blankets of her bed. Where is she? Where could she be?

Someone was walking slowly down the hall. I knew who it was by the way she held her head up and her shoulders back. The light bulb at the top of the stairs made her hazy and grainy, like a picture out of focus.

"Hello, Amory," Cady said.

The sides of my stomach squeezed in then out. Felt like I'd managed to touch a bare wire and the current was racing every which way, trying to find a way out. "Hi."

"Happy birthday." Her eyes wandered over me, taking in just by looking. "I have something for you."

I watched her standing framed in the doorway, jacket over her arm. "May I hold you, just for a minute?" As she leaned against me, I could feel how her body had curved with mine in the dark last night.

"Do you want your present?" she asked, moving away.

I nodded.

"Then come on." Cady stepped by me and went up the stairs. I took a deep breath and followed.

My room took up the east end of the attic and at least it was clean. Cady sat on the floor, shoes off. I noticed her socks; one was white and the other blue and yellow argyle.

"So where is it?" I asked, sitting down Indian style next to her.

Cady dug a bottle from under her jacket and handed it over.

"Cheap champagne. I love it." I really did, even if it only cost three bucks a bottle. I started unpeeling the foil.

"I have something else for you, too."

"Oh, yeah?" I looked up from twisting the wire. I didn't need a corkscrew since the cork was plastic.

"I'll give it to you in a minute. I want to talk first."

I started pulling at the cork, twisting it to get it loose. The bottle was so cold it made my hands ache. "What about?"

"Last night."

The cork was far enough to push it the rest of the way with my thumbs. "Yeah?"

"Yeah."

It flew off, smacking the middle of my Judy Chicago poster and landing on the blue shag rug near my feet. "Want a glass?" I asked, holding up the bottle.

"Listen, Ames, I'm really serious."

"I know, Cady, I know you are." I took a drink and handed the champagne to her. She drank a little, watching me the whole time. I grabbed the cork and tossed it from hand to hand. The damn thing was hollow. I flipped it into the air and it bounced on the rug again.

"I loved waking up with you."

These socks were getting pretty thin at each of the big toes. I was going to have to wear them upside-down.

"I really did," she went on. "I liked it so much I want to do it again."

Somebody turned up the juice, the current getting hotter as it slamdanced under my skin. I bounced my leg a few times then wrapped my arms around my knees. She looked at me, the bottle on the floor in front of her and her hands laced together in her lap.

"I want to be your lover, Amory."

I stretched out my legs and pulled them back.

"I want to touch you so much." Her voice was low and husky, like too many cigarettes had carved a way down her throat.

I slugged champagne, enough so when it foamed up none ran out the top.

"Ames, God, I don't want to scare you."

I tied two loose threads together that hung from the cuff of my jeans. "I told you I was done being scared,

136

Cady," I said, feeling like I was against a wire-woven fence, each single diamond pushing into my back.

"Maybe this isn't the right time or place to talk about this." She twisted her ring, the gold looking flat and dull since there was only one good bulb left in the light fixture. "I better go."

She was halfway to her feet. I grabbed her hand and pulled her back to the floor. "No. Please." I added, "Please don't go. We can talk about whatever you want, I don't care. I want you to stay, that's what I want for my birthday." I kissed her, surprising both of us, trying to tell her I wanted, wanted, wanted — what? Wanted her? Wanted to shut the door and turn out the light and pretend we were the only people left in the world? Pulling away, I spoke again. "I lied."

"When?"

"I am scared."

She smiled.

"I am so scared I don't think there are words big enough to tell you." My hands fell away from her shoulders, leaving only our knees touching.

"So am I, hon."

"I've never done this before, Cady. I'm not very pretty and you're beautiful and I don't want to screw everything up —"

"Amory." She put her hands on my face.

"But what if I'm terrible at this?" Fear bit me at the back of the neck. Oh shit, what have I got into this time?

"Terrible at what? At making love with me? Whenever we're together, when we laugh or talk —" Her musical laugh sent sparks up my back, "or take a walk, all those times, Amory, we make love. I want to fall into bed with you because we already share all those things.

137

Because I want to tell you things with my hands, tell you that you're sweet and sexy and exciting and that I love you."

"You love me?" It felt strange in my mouth to say such things.

"I've been wanting to tell you since the day I first asked you for a cigarette and you ran away."

"Do you know what I did? I ran to Daniel to find out who the hell you were."

"He told you?"

"Of course. Even said I could take it as a compliment. You had me terrified for weeks, thinking that I looked like a queer girl. I could've shot you for the misery. I spent a lot of time getting Daniel away from his typewriter and into the loving arms and legs of his woman." I snorted. "Shit."

"All to prove you weren't a baby dyke?"

I nodded. Somehow being a baby dyke didn't look so bad after all.

"If I knew my asking you for a cigarette was going to throw you into a sexual existential crisis —"

"— you would've sent flowers to speed up the whole thing."

"Ames, I'm shocked,"she managed to get out between giggles.

"You lie like a rug, Cady Baird. There I was sweet and innocent, well, maybe not innocent, but not exactly ready for kinky shit and you sidle up to proposition me on the steps of the Admin Building."

"I did not proposition you. I was simply trying to charm you. Get your interest."

"Hell." I smiled. I must've looked pretty stupid sitting there with my jaw flapping in the breeze.

"Worked, didn't it?"

138

I laughed with her a little bit, looking at the place where my knee touched hers. Her jeans were more faded, each single line of chalky blue distinct from the others. "Yeah, yep, yep, yep."

She gave me massage oil, to rub on my body, she said, lighting my birthday candle. I turned out the light, leaving us in cinnamon red as we kissed, mouths and clothes loosening while people downstairs celebrated my birthday.

"I'm twenty-two today, Cady."

"I know. Just a baby."

Her hands move, leaving a coat of oil that smelled musky on warm bare skin. I was afraid to move, afraid to lose the touch of her, caught watching the wall and her shadow moving across it.

"This feels good?" I could hear her smiling.

A deep rumble echoed in my throat as I lay beneath her hands and thighs. I was purring like a cat as she stretched muscles for me.

"I'll take that as a yes." She kissed between my shoulder blades, making me twitch all over in an electric way. Kneading my arms, she moved further up my back, and I could feel her hair in the same place she had kissed me.

I turned my head. "I can feel you, in the middle of my back, right behind my heart."

"Do you want me to move?" Her hands stopped again.

"Could you sit up a minute? A little higher."

She lifted up, giving me just enough room to turn over. I slipped my hands up her arms to her shoulders and around her neck. The flame of the candle turned her nipples almost brown and the rest of her deep gold.

Cady loves me; I could see it in the curve of her body. I squeezed my eyes shut for a second to engrave this picture

139

in my mind. She was soft and round and strong. I kissed her, feeling her stretch out lean and curved on top of me, our thighs braiding.

We carried on like trash until the candle hissed out and the sun began edging into the sky. I swept back a corner of the curtain to look outside. Everything red and gold in autumn looked brown as river mud. Soon, the sun would turn the morning sky deep blue and the leaves into a rush of color. Cady bit my shoulder, then ran her tongue down my neck, making every part of me fit where her mouth touched. She traced her fingers across my belly soft as morning sliding into the sky.

* * * * *

"This and this and this," I muttered, stacking the pages into a folder for McClure. Need a new ribbon, some different paper, and a dictionary because I can't spell worth shit. Paper-clipping one batch, I chucked it in with the good work, then out again. It was sex stuff and there was a burn through all of them because I finished it right when Cady peeled off my shirt and I thought I put my cigarette in the ashtray but missed by a mile. Might've been burned to death if we hadn't smelled the smoke.

* * * * *

"I can't believe you've never heard Jill sing." McClure was excited. She was two steps ahead of me going through the door.

"I never paid attention to when she was playing," I said, catching the door before it swung back and knocked me flat on my ass. McClure stood inside, looking around Angelo's for an empty table.

140

"Where's the best place to sit?"

"Hell, lady, I don't know. I've only been here once before." I scanned the dark and pointed to a corner. McClure followed me to a table across from a speaker.

"I remember when I was a junior and working summer grounds crew," she began as I hung my jacket on the back of a chair and rubbed my arms. I'd gotten a little chilly on the way over; she promised to buy me a poncho just like hers, said I'd never get cold wearing it. "All the orientation people were supposed to put on a talent show in the basement of the chapel." We both sat down, feet up on two other chairs so no one else would grab them from us. "Detroit LaRue was running the whole thing and since I was madly in lust for her at the time, I went, too."

"Detroit LaRue? Who's that?" The bar was about halfway full and I could tell the drunk boys in the baseball caps were looking forward to the evening; they had a pyramid of empty beer bottles stacked on their table.

"You remind me of Detroit a lot. Same high cheek-bones, same blue eyes, though she looked almost Asian since her eyes were almond-shaped. Correction: eye was almond-shaped. She wore an eyepatch."

"Eyepatch? Did she need it or did she just wear it?" I didn't seen Angelo serving drinks, so I figured it was up to me to go to the bar.

"She needed it. The left one was missing. God, she was something, got everybody high a couple times, did insane things. She disappeared a couple years ago the same time Angel did. I heard she found Jesus and joined a cult. Either that or she became a revolutionary in Nicaragua."

"And I remind you of her? Great. I got the aura of a born-again who smuggles drugs. I've been wondering what labels to wear these days, McClure."

141

"You reminded me of her, that's all. You have the same kind of body and almost the same kind of hair, except hers is lighter and she has a tiny braid with glass beads strung through it that goes to the middle of her back. But you move differently. Her shoulders are always tight, like she's carrying a secret. You walk like you know where your feet are."

"I do. They're at the end of my legs."

"Funny. You're quite a comedian. Anyway, during this talent show, this little monkey-like woman walked onto the stage carrying this beat-up guitar and everybody started squirming in their seats thinking this better be mercifully quick. Then she started playing. They wouldn't let her leave."

Cady stood before us, coat in hand. "Hi, women."

Standing up, I managed to brush off my surprise. I hadn't heard or seen her come up to the table. Her arms closed around me in a tight hug. We pressed together. I could hear each breath she took in my ear, the warmth lightly slipping through my hair to the nape of my neck, sending tingles of another surprise.

"You smell like women touching."

My insides went to water.

She sat down just as Rhys came in as noisy as Cady'd been quiet, her hurried moves rasping against the whispered feeling between Cady and me. Angelo's began to fill after that, but despite more noise I could hear Cady's soft, confident, you smell like women touching. I should. I'd touched her not more than three hours ago, this woman, the heat of her now passing through skin and into me as we sat at a small, square table. I smell like us, a lurking scent ready to curve into escape. I hadn't taken a shower, didn't wash away her fingerprints on my skin. It felt deliciously illegal, like if the FBI dusted me from head to toe for fingerprints they'd find some mighty suspicious marks in some mighty interesting places.

Jill came out, said hello then sat at another table full of admirers. Cady gazed around the room, and between a tangled conversation with McClure and Rhys, chatted with people who stopped by. I pretended to do the same thing, though this afternoon came back to start a fire where the line of her leg met mine. Soon, the lights around the edge of the stage grew brighter and everyone crowded around. It got quiet enough to hear the hum of the sound system. Jill stood up from her chair, drank the last of a glass of beer and walked to the stage.

For the first time I actually liked what was coming out of her mouth as she blasted away on her guitar and sang more colors than the blues. Jess would've liked this, especially "Jambalaya." She liked Hank Williams — all of her records were him, Marty Robbins or religious crap. She used to always say that anything else, except Peggy Lee, was about lust and drugs, especially that rock and roll, so she never let me have my own stereo. Jessie was right about metal music, but even when I was forced to hear Tennessee Ernie Ford all I thought about was lust and drugs anyway.

About halfway through the first set the beer bottle pyramid collapsed. The guys had been banging on the table in applause.

* * * * *

"It's good, some of it." McClure opened the file and looked at me standing across the table.

"Some of it?"

"Yeah. If you can cut out the best and fit what goes together, you'll have some decent first pieces."

143

"Decent? Fuck decent. I want to be great."

"For someone who hasn't been writing very long, decent is pretty good, Amory."

"But not excellent?"

She considered it. "No."

"Not fabulous?"

She shook her head and shuffled the pages. "No."

"Not even magnificent?"

McClure grinned. "Sorry."

"Then I quit." I crossed my arms and stamped my foot. But somewhere inside all the messing around, it hurt to hear I hadn't blown her away.

"Your endings are incredible, the middle sections do what they have to do, but you have no beginnings, nothing to start from. You have to get grounded in something, Amory, find someplace to put your feet. You need to remember specific detail. Say what you see. Make every word count."

I stared at her and chewed on a paperclip, the way a hick would chew a weed. "Yeah," I said. "Yeah."

* * * * *

Morning always came too early after winter blew in, giving each black reaching hand of the trees a white glove of snow that looked like a backwards shadow. The unlit street would stare into my room; I would shield myself from the cold wind with a single wool blanket and my typewriter. Working, working, trying for a first line, some sort of beginning. Sometimes the snow would rush from the sky, hitting the window like someone had thrown a handful of perfect white beads against the glass.

Mornings I woke with Cady, the air smelling like ice and burnt wood, curled around her like a spoon with her hips tucked against my thighs. Our clothes would be scattered in knots around her bed, the sounds she makes when I touch her echoing in my mind. Some days we stayed there, to make love and share warmth, and some days we'd race for a shower, dress as quick as we could, and meet Rhys and McClure in the Center to talk and laugh and argue.

"Sometimes my dad would read to us before we went to bed." McClure was slumped so low in her chair I could only see her eyes over the table littered with coffee cups and books. "There's a great big chair in the living room, not one of those recliners, but a big overstuffed one with dark brown upholstery. It's really pretty ugly, now that I think about it. But we'd all sit in his lap, Jamie and me and Derek and Tina, with my Dad underneath trying to hold the book up so he could read it and all of us see the pictures."

"I remember one about the three beans," Cady said, elbows on the table.

"What the hell is that one," I asked, "I never heard of it before."

"It's like the three pigs but different," explained Rhys, trying to twist her shirt collar into the right shape. I don't think she ever learned to iron from the way her clothes always look.

"There was one that scared the shit out of me," McClure went on. "The one about the little girl who wanted a pair of red shoes. That's all she wanted, and when she finally got them and put them on her feet, she couldn't stop dancing and died. It's a ballet and a movie, I think."

"Great thing to show your kids."

"Well, hell, they're all like that, Cady. Somebody gets eaten up or mangled or turned into a horrible monster."

145

"Or put to sleep and can't wake up till a handsome prince kisses her," Rhys added.

I scratched the back of my neck. "Yeah, I guess that's pretty horrible."

"Did you ever read the Mrs. Pigglewiggle books? I read the first one when I was in fourth, no, third grade. It was third grade because I had Mrs. Becker."

"You had your third grade teacher?" Cady's eyebrow shot up and she reached for my cigarettes. "My, my, I've heard of lesbian thoughts surfacing at that tender age, but never did I hear of an eight-year-old baby dyke getting that kind of action."

"Get your mind out of the gutter, Baird. You astound me by the way you can find sex in everything."

She lit a match. "I find it because it's there, McClure."

"Hey, I remember Mrs. Pigglewiggle. She had the upside-down house." I could almost see the little sketch of it.

"You and Sigmund Freud could take over the world by scaring people into insane asylums. You'd find the sex and he'd tell them they're sick."

"I think Freud did fine all by himself," Cady murmured.

"Do you remember the one story where the little girl is so dirty that Mrs. Pigglewiggle tells her mom to plant magic seeds on her and the next day there's a radish growing out of her head?" I sat up in my chair. It was like I'd checked them out of the library just last week, I could remember those books so well.

"Does anyone want another cup of coffee?" Rhys broke in.

"Yes." McClure dug into her jeans for money. "How about you, Ames? It's on me."

"Sure."

Cady shook her head and took a drag as Rhys walked away.

I'd read those books. They were my favorites after *Harriet the Spy*.

* * * * *

The light of the sun was broken by the bamboo shades on the window, the pieces falling on me in bed. Somewhere I'd heard a phone ringing, now stopped. I rolled over.

"Hi."

I shoved the pillows under my head. "You know, one of us is going to have to break down and change the sheets."

"Are you volunteering?" She smiled and leaned against the doorframe.

"Hell, no." I hunted for my cigarettes; found them near my tennis shoes with a book of matches stuck in the cellophane wrapper. "What time is it?"

"Around one," she said, tightening the belt of her robe then sliding her hands in the pockets to pull the blue-black plaid down the front of her.

I lit up, dropping the burnt match on the foil under the candles. They were on a small shelf near the futon, along with a bottle of oil, a tube of KY, and the silver chain she'd worn that first night. I picked it up. It was a tiny chain, fragile, in a pattern called serpentine. I dropped it onto the wood. "I'm hungry."

"Really?"

"Really." The cigarette burned in my left hand. I lay on my back, pillows behind my head, the places where the sun hit the sheet turning almost too white. The light streaks of the room striped Cady's eyes; I could feel her gaze on my skin as she followed the pale shadows in the bed.

"You are stunning, lying there like that."

The touch of her echoed to my bones and back. I watched the blue smoke of the cigarette string its way in the black shadows to the ceiling, each strand long and round and perfect. The ember faded to nothing in the light. The sun never seemed to shine so bright as it did here. Skies I spent most of my time under were sanded gray by burning coal.

"What are you thinking about?"

"Back in Sterling, the Macons are so stingy they wouldn't give you daylight if they could keep it off you."

"What made you think of them?"

"Greedy people have long arms; they were tapping me on the shoulder." I smiled up at her. The strength of her legs and arms filled her, the muscles rounding under her skin. She was pinks and whites. I was browns and tans. Memory filled my hands, feeling her sweetness like cotton candy melting all over me, feeling the half-moons of her spine and the edges of shoulderblades in my fingers.

She walked across the room. "I love you."

It echoed between strips of light and dark.

I flicked an ash into the foil as she came toward me.

"I do, you know."

"You'd almost have to."

She took my cigarette, inhaled then blew out a corona of smoke. "Why is it so hard for you to understand?"

"It isn't. Who wouldn't be in love with me? I'm a fucking genius."

"I'm serious."

"I know." I took my cigarette. "It's just that I don't know how you can be."

"It's natural. Like breathing."

"Well, we all have our own little weirdnesses."

She flashed a smile like a kid's. "Have any you'd like to share?"

I shook my head and watched her sitting on the edge of the bed, her hair flashing more to gold than auburn, her robe curving open to show the tops of her breasts.

She asked, "Have you ever played cat's cradle?"

"When I was little, like in grade school. Me and Tara Maple were the best."

Cady picked up a hunk of string laying by the bed. "Want to play?"

"Where did you get that?"

"Off Joe Don's shoe box."

I stuck the cigarette into the corner of my mouth to make me look tough, like a pool hustler. "You sure you want to play with me, toots?"

As she looped the string through her fingers to make the cradle, the stray lumps and knots flew around and got in the way.

"Not going to work, huh?" she asked me, looking over the clots.

I shook my head, spinning the filter down to grip in my front teeth so I could wiggle the cigarette up and down.

Cady broke the string, the sound dry like chicken bones snapping, tearing out the knots. "For this game, it's all a question of tying the perfect knot," she said, wrists and fingers tightening and yanking and pulling.

"Cady?"

"Uh huh?" She was intent on getting her knot. "Look at this," she said, holding up the string, "this is a pretty good one. Except for the loose ends."

"Who was on the phone?"

"You can't trim the extra, that's cheating."

149

"Cady —"

Re-tying to get the ends shorter, she looked at me.

"Who called?"

"When?"

"Just a little while ago. Who was it?"

"McClure."

"For me?"

"I didn't want to wake you. You didn't get to sleep until late." She leaned over and kissed me, the knotting forgotten in her hands.

I blew a smoke ring. "What did she want?"

"Just wondering where you were. I told her you were here, safe and sound." She tossed the string aside. "You don't believe me?"

Believe? I don't believe anything. And I don't believe in anything, either. Funny how one little word can change somebody's question.

"Hey there? It wasn't a philosophical question. You do trust me, don't you?"

"Sure, yeah, of course I do. I just keep getting lost in my head." Faith, truth, the answer to the universe. I'll be damned but that I'll find all the answers I need right in my own backyard just like Dorothy in *The Wizard of Oz*.

"Amory?"

"Yeah?" Shit, I did it again, went wandering in my mind in the middle of a conversation.

"Happy anniversary."

"Anniversary?"

"Four months."

"Oh, yeah. Sure." I never kept track of such things.

"Because of this auspicious occasion, you're getting the greatest breakfast of your life or at least the greatest you've ever had in my house. Be back in a flash."

150

We ate bagels and peanut butter in bed. The champagne that spilled was covered by a towel and Cady crowded my side, her back to the window, smoking a cigarette. She'd rolled the shade up so the sun covered us through the bare winter trees.

"Your hair is almost black here," she said, uncurling some from the triangle.

"Except where the scar is. Ain't any grow on it." I chewed the last of my bagel. I don't think I like them after all, slick and rubbery in my mouth.

Cady put her cigarette out. "Does it hurt?"

I felt her hand on my belly. "No." I squished the cigarette butt down some more to make sure it was out and set the ashtray back on the floor.

"What did Jessie say about it? About how you got it?"

"Bad things happen to bad people."

"But it's not your fault —"

"I know that," I said quietly. "But how am I to tell Jess now? Go into a trance? I hate that ouija board shit." I laughed and pulled her closer. "Would you ever shave your pubic hair?" She hadn't shaved anywhere for almost three years.

"Jesus, that's quite a jump, isn't it?"

"I just have different things on my mind than you do, that's all. So would you?"

"Hell, no. Why? Do you have fantasies about it?" Cady squirmed and put her arm around my waist.

"Uh uh. I don't think I'd like it. Be like touching a little girl or playing with a hard-boiled egg."

"I know someone who did that once. He shaved his hair off because it was blonde and nobody could see it."

"Did he cut himself?" I reached for the bowl of fruit Cady had brought up. I grabbed an apple and put it back. I don't like to eat them unless they're sliced; little pieces get caught in my teeth and make my gums bleed.

"I didn't ask."

"I thought maybe you saw a band-aid coming out of his drawers." I got a banana this time and started unpeeling it.

"Jesus," Cady laughed, laying flat on her back. "Your timing is perfect."

"What do you mean?" I asked between chews.

"Lying in bed with a naked woman and you're eating a banana. Freud would have a field day."

"Good thing we didn't invite Freud."

* * * * *

"I know this guy who has nodules on his vocal cords because he's six-foot-four and thinks he should have this butch bass voice. He's normally a tenor."

"The guy is an asshole," I said to Cady.

"Turns out he is," she conceded, "but I think what he did is proof that men are pushed into molds just as often as women."

"No one is arguing that isn't true," Rhys pointed out. "But middle-class white men gain much more by conformity because they thought of the definitions."

"Better be careful. I know some people who'd like to see all the boys launched into outer space." McClure snuck a grin at me, then stuffed the last of her granola bar into her mouth. I don't know how she can stand those things but she eats them like a machine. When we walked into the snack bar a few minutes ago, the woman at the counter had three on a little paper plate ready for her.

152

"Bullshit on that noise. Separatism is a head game. If we all practice it we'll end up being monkeys throwing nuts at each other out of different trees."

"I don't think you should insult monkeys like that," Rhys murmured, sitting back in her chair.

"I read something about monkeys," I began, trying to remember, "in *National Geographic* or *National Enquirer* or something. You know how monkeys scratch at themselves like they're looking for bugs? They're not. They're looking for salt crystals caught in their fur from being in the hot jungle."

"Monkey sweat. Delicious," Rhys threw back.

"Jessie made me drink salt water once. I threw up all day. If I'm ever shipwrecked I know enough not to drink out of the sea. I was sick as a dog."

"Hey, would you listen to me for a second, please?" Cady begged.

"Did you drink gasoline or something? You give somebody salt water if they've been poisoned. I think. Right?" McClure turned to Rhys. "Sure it is. I read that in *The Reader's Digest Medical Dictionary.*"

"You don't give them salt water, you give them milk," Cady answered. "It depends on what kind of poison it is. Sometimes they give you stuff so you throw up —"

"Does anybody want some more coffee?" I asked, sorry I'd started the conversation. I'd rather talk about monkeys. They all shook their heads.

Walking to the front counter, I could see my jeep parked half on the sidewalk. I was going to have to move it or I was going to get me a ticket.

"Even lesbians enforce body types," McClure spoke angrily as I walked to the table. "Butches wear leather

153

and femmes wear three-inch heel victim shoes, remember?"

"We used to call them slut shoes," I said, setting down my cup as the three of them turned. "People in Sterling are proud to be members of the unwashed masses."

"That's shit," Cady went on. "Not one of us fits those two stereotypes. We fit others."

I blew on my coffee and glanced around. Rhys's expression was blank, making her look as cold and brittle as a stiletto. A look of disgust twisted McClure's open, smooth face, and her arms were crossed tight in front of her.

"Look at you McClure, funky earth-mother, and you Rhys, the gray-streaked straight-haired, lean-jawed intellectual. And me, half softball dyke —"

"And half lezzie sex goddess," I broke in. I bit the styrofoam cup, leaving teethmarks.

"Then there's Amory," she said.

"Huh?" McClure and Rhys stared at me. "I don't want to be no dyke pin-up girl."

"Look at that face," Cady went on, her voice sounding like she was doing a commercial, "that bone structure, deep ice-blue eyes you'd love to fall into, yet seem to scare you to death because no one knows what's behind them, all framed with that dark, almost black hair. The perfect androgyne. And that's only her face." She leaned over to kiss me.

My stomach tightened like I'd swallowed a rock and I pulled away. "Don't do that."

"Hey," she half-laughed, then began to sing softly, *"You must remember this,"* she moved, close enough that I was ready for her mouth to touch mine, *"a kiss is just a kiss —"*

"Quit playing boy games, Cady."

154

I snapped my head to McClure. Her jaw was clenched, the muscle bulging up just like Bobby Lee's used to when he was losing at pool. Funny, I hadn't thought of him for years.

"What?" Cady wasn't surprised. She was shocked.

"She asked you not to and she meant it."

"I think Amory can make her own decisions, McClure. Besides, I wasn't going to do anything," she answered with a sudden disarming smile.

"You're lying."

"Getting a little personal, aren't you?" Cady's voice went tight and cool, smile gone as quick as it'd shown up.

"You play with truth the way kids play with gum; you stretch it, rearrange it, then drop it on the sidewalk to stick to someone else's shoe and be someone else's problem." She shook her head over and over. "You really think you have it all, don't you?"

"Of course. Even you would have to admit that." The words slip-knotted, catching McClure in them.

I reached for my cigarettes. Jesus Christ, what did I miss on my way to get coffee? Cady ran her hand through her hair, deliberate and slow so's to show she wasn't upset or angry or anything. I lit up, blowing out hard. Rhys pushed the ashtray over though it was plenty close enough for me to reach it, and by her look I knew this was going to last awhile.

"Did you ever think maybe you were wrong?"

"Once, maybe," Cady took my cigarette and inhaled. "But I was mistaken."

I'd never seen McClure angry, never. Even when somebody got drunk at one of her parties and threw the little vase she got in China against the wall for no reason. She just picked up the pieces and brought them to the Art Building to glue them back together.

"You are one of the most selfish people I have ever met."

"Guilty as charged."

"She said no, and you don't give a damn. You'll use anybody to get what you want, won't you Cady?"

"What exactly do you mean by that?" Cady asked, as quiet as McClure was loud.

"Come on, you two, that's enough," Rhys finally refereed.

"You think you have the right to collect people like pretty things you can amuse yourself with. You eat people up. Never give them anything back and toss them out at the first convenient second."

"Better watch it, McClure. You're mixing your metaphors."

I looked at my coffee. It left brown rings on the inside of the cup.

"Now, I don't know what's up your ass," Cady went on, diplomatic as hell, "but I think you're finished right now."

"Maybe you should listen for once," she snapped. "You might learn something."

"Really? About what?" Her eyebrows arched.

"About how Ames needs some time alone, needs other writers, needs to get some work done, not your superficial —"

"Why don't you just admit that you can't stand the fact that I'm sleeping with Amory and you're not?"

My chair fell over to bounce on the floor. The double doors slammed out against the wall. I headed down the hall. Had to get out, had to get away, had to run away. It was like high school when Jennifer Garther started talking so loud I could hear what she was saying about me to a bunch of her friends.

156

"Amory!"

How fucking dare they?

"Amory! Wait!"

I slowed down a little for Rhys. She hadn't done anything to piss me off, no reason to take it out on her. She walked behind me, I could hear her over my shoulder. I stopped suddenly and she almost walked into me.

"Doesn't having people hanging all over bug the shit out of you?"

"Sometimes," she answered me as we stood in the middle of the hall.

"Would drive me batshit."

"Amory." She touched my arm. "Would you come back and sit down with me?"

"No."

"We'll sit somewhere else, not with those two."

She led me back to the study lounge. The couches were ugly, green with mustard-yellow and ketchup-red lines running through them. Every time we had coffee out here I felt like I was sitting on a huge rotting hot dog.

"I think I know what happened back there."

"Yeah? So do I. They were acting like shitheads."

She smiled reluctantly, and sat up on the edge of the couch. "I understand how you feel, in fact, I agree with you. But there is a reason for it."

"No, there isn't."

Rhys sighed. "Ames —"

I waited as she gathered her words together.

"Cady and McClure, well, until you entered the picture, they sort of ignored each other."

"What does that have to do with it?"

"Please, Amory, don't make this difficult. Things don't just happen, there's always a trigger."

"And where there's a Trigger, there's Roy Rogers." It was meant to be a joke and didn't sound like one at all.

She ignored it. "Look, the two of them have been competitors for a while, always testing each other. You're a beautiful woman, just as Cady said. You're also something of a mystery to a lot of people, very magnetic, very attractive, and I think McClure is tired of getting baited."

"What the hell do you mean? I'm no mystery girl."

"To McClure, Cady just won the battle. And she has a nasty habit of flaunting the trophy."

"I'm not the grand prize for whoever can knock all the tin cans over."

"Maybe McClure wants a Vita Sackville-West to her Virginia Woolf, Alice B. to Gertrude, Una to Radclyffe." She spread her arms out like a fan.

"Una who?"

She sighed again, this time disgusted with my ignorance. "McClure wants a teammate."

The idea slowly drifted like feathers in a wind and settled in my thoughts. "She wants me to be Robin to her Batman?"

"Right."

My ears started to buzz, and I mean really buzz, like mosquitos were stuck in my hair. "I don't play second to nobody."

"I know," she said gently. "But I think Cady may have pushed McClure to the breaking point."

"Wait a second. Are you trying to tell me McClure is jealous?"

"Well —"

"That's it, right?"

Rhys said nothing.

"I'll be goddamned. McClure." I stared at the tile floor. It doesn't make any sense, McClure is the one everybody knows, she's the one everybody likes.

"Amory?"

I raised my head. She stood there, next to Rhys, her fists clenched at her sides.

"I think it's only fair that you hear me out, Ames," she said in her McClure-the-righteous-poet voice I'd heard once before at a reading. I hated it. So much I swore I'd never go to another one till she learned to talk like herself.

I don't want to hear this. I put my hand up. "Don't say anything, McClure. Just don't say anything."

I went into the Center. Cady sat at the table, finishing my cigarette or else smoking a new one. I grabbed the half-empty pack resting near her hand; reading upside down, Marlboro looks like Maddog. "Do you want any to take with you?" I lit a cigarette, watching the smoke of the dead match disappear into the air.

"No. Do you want to sit down?"

"No." I slung my backpack over my shoulder and walked away. "No."

"I'll call you later," she called after me.

* * * * *

I ran all the way from class to my jeep, trying to miss the bigger puddles. A campus cop was just about to stick a ticket under the windshield wiper when I jumped in and roared out of the president's parking spot. I ended up parked in the fucking middle of nowhere.

Need a cup of coffee. I went to the Center, taking the steps two at a time, my tennis shoes run-down enough to be slippery on the tile especially where the water had

159

gathered from the melting slush. I'd forgotten my coat hanging on the back of my desk; the March wind had frozen my skin and shoved my hair into my face with one roar. Been a couple of crummy days. At least I don't have a nine buck parking ticket on top of it.

"Hi," someone said from above me.

I raked my hair out of my eyes with my fingers. The same tight smile behind a different beard. He'd shaved the hair on his face into a goatee and moustache. It looked horrible.

"Just the person I've been wanting to see."

Fuck. "Not now, Daniel."

"It's important."

"Is it about my furniture?"

He looked at his shoes and blushed. At least Daniel Jacobson had enough conscience to be embarrassed. "Uh, no."

"Then me and you have nothing to talk about."

He tapped the toe of his boot against the floor as I walked up the stairs. "I really wish we could be friends."

"Well, you can wish in one hand and shit in the other and see which one gets full first."

"Christ, Amory, I'm really trying to say I'm sorry."

"Cut the crap, I'm not in the mood to hear it."

Daniel looked at me as if I'd slapped him so hard his little red beret had spun off his head.

"You know, you have this ability to show up at all the wrong times to say all the wrong things. It's a gift you have." The words shot out, fired by anger. For a second, I wanted to strangle him, strangle somebody, just shut the whole world up so I could think. I held my breath, letting it out slowly, and turned to leave.

"Amory?" He got between me and the doors. "Would you please think about giving our friendship a chance?"

160

His hand reached out like there was no bullshit, no hard feelings. Forget Cady or me going into movies; he had us both beat.

"What's the matter, your latest sixteen-year-old dump you on your head?"

His eyes narrowed. "Are you going to drag all that up again? I've changed, Amory."

Daniel was five-eight and if I stood up straight I could look him right in the eye. "Sure you have, Daniel."

"I have. But there's one thing that hasn't changed; I still love you." His voice was soft, greasy with how easy it came out of him.

"You're lying, just like before."

"I got hurt then, too, you know."

"Ain't that too bad?" I looked at his eyes. I used to think them warm and deep. They were hard and flat now, like an oil slick. "I don't care if you've changed, I don't care if you've grown up, I don't care if you've become a sensitive man. I don't like you." The sides of my stomach tightened, sending a hard knot in a fury of direction to my edges.

His sneer turned his face crooked and ugly. "But you like those lesbians, don't you?"

Steady. No need to be as bad as he is. I pulled out a cigarette, trying to get control. The match scratched, louder than usual. "That's none of your goddamn business, now is it?" I said it the same way I would say have a happy day.

"Everybody knows exactly how much you like Cady Baird. In fact, we all know you've turned into a dyke, too."

Cady. I wonder where she is. I blew a smoke ring he waved away.

"Why did you go gay, Ames? Did I hurt you that much?" Daniel stepped closer, his voice dropping so low I could hardly hear him except for its echoing in the stairwell. "I can make it up to you."

My back went tight, shoulders shifting and tensing as he stared. He wouldn't try anything here, not where his friends could find out.

"The sex couldn't be better than what we had." He was close enough that I could see the threads weaving back and forth in his jacket, each going crisscrossed. "When we made love . . ." His voice trailed away.

Too close, he was standing too close. I had to get to the door. I clenched my keys in my fist, the metal teeth biting the skin between each finger.

"Everybody's talking about you, I try to stop them, but some things just can't be stopped, you know?" He was so close I could feel the breath behind each word. "We can be friends, Amory, good friends. I can make you forget Cady Baird."

"I doubt it," I said, blowing a lungful of smoke at his face.

Daniel coughed and turned away. I stepped around him and through the door.

* * * * *

I tossed my jacket on the floor and walked across the room. Disembodied voices echoed in the living room from the TV set as soon as I pulled out the knob. I clicked through the channels, stopping once when the gray screen lit up with colors unbending into the faces. I turned it off. I hate television. The room got real quiet, not even noise from outside could make a dent. I flopped onto the sofa. Maybe I should get a cat. Or a gerbil. Would be homey to walk in the door and hear the happy little squeaks of the gerbil-wheel spinning and spinning. They don't eat much either.

Damn him. Why did he think he had the right to stomp into my life anytime he had an inkling? Thought I'd never have to deal with him ever again, if he ever bothers me again I swear I won't be responsible for what happens. I'll feed him to my new pet.

Maybe McClure isn't here. I haven't seen her for two days, not since I told her to leave me alone. She did. I hear her getting up in the morning for classes and when I go downstairs I find a pot of coffee she's left for me, though I end up dumping it because I don't have time for even one cup. That's the only trace of her.

What about that mess? She's my friend, but what if it was only because Cady was in the scene, or maybe Cady was because of McClure? What if neither gives two fucks about me? That isn't true, I know it isn't. McClure is my friend. She gave me a place to live and books to read and I can use her electric typewriter whenever I want. I'm sick to death of thinking about it. It's like the two of them just up and left me.

Loneliness knocked at the back of my head, the old feeling of standing on an ice island. I could almost see it, a big, beautiful castle like the one that sank the Titanic, huge and floating the North Pole with me as the only inhabitant. No one can get near for fear of being sunk. I glanced around the room, the walls seeming to stretch beyond the house. I don't know why it's like being on an ice floe. I've never been much interested in such places, just once I read something about an expedition that'd been caught trying to get through Northern Canada in the nineteenth century. Some explorers found one of the guys who died at the beginning, a sailor named John

Torrington who had tuberculosis. They'd been trying to figure out what happened to the expedition and they dug him up. He was a hundred years old and all I could think was how sad it was that they had left him alone in the tundra, buried there all by himself.

My eyes started to sting. I blinked twice. That was what this was like. Breathe deep, slow, it'd been a long time since being left on ice. Months. Since living with McClure. She didn't deny what Cady had said about me.

Cady. How does this love shit get started? How could she look at me with a glint in her eye that seemed to pin me to the floor?

"Hey." McClure was wearing her glasses and old sweats, which meant she was reading in bed. She stood in the hallway looking at me.

"Hey, yourself. What you doing?"

"Lying around getting over a yeast infection." She smiled softly. "How about you?"

I just looked at the floor.

"I'm reading some of the new poetry you gave me. The Joanna Nobody poems. Have you thought about what I said? About your first lines?"

"Yeah," I answered, not really giving two hoots and a go to hell.

"And?"

"Seems all the time I end up smack in the middle of things and stay behind till the very end. First lines? Don't got any. Have no beginnings. If I do, I got nowhere to learn them from. Can't ask Jess."

"There are other ways."

"Dead is dead, McClure."

"If you don't know the facts, dream them up."

"Dream?"

"Why not?"

164

"And that's it?"

"If it's all you have, Ames."

"It ain't the nature of a dream to last a lifetime."

"But a dream will work for these poems. Who is Joanna Nobody?"

"Somebody I think I should know."

"A facet of yourself you haven't met?"

"I don't know. Maybe. I found her photograph in Jessie's book. I feel like I should know her, or at least her real name."

"I gathered that from the poems. When they work, Ames, Joanna Nobody haunts the room, even without strong first lines."

Joanna's face came clear to me, not as a picture, but in real life — the cheekbones, the hair and the pearl she wore that she reached up to touch with one finger. Who is she? At least she could tell me. Slowly, Joanna's face dissolved, leaving traces like chalk on a sidewalk after the rain.

McClure and I watched one another in the quiet room.

"Amory?" She edged toward the couch and sat down next to me. "I really want to say I'm sorry." Her voice was the same as the day she introduced herself at the table the first time we drank coffee together.

"It's okay," I managed. I got out a cigarette and lit up into my own private fog.

McClure's fingers lay gently on my shoulder and then she slid her arm around. Tears stung again. I peered through the smoke screen at her and knew what she would look like when she got very, very old.

"Let do what's been done, McClure." I spoke softly, watching tears trace silver lines down her face. Jessie used to say that, when no fixing could help.

Damn dream.

I sat up in bed. Blankets crowded my waist. Wind pushed against the window, a shivering, loose sound like teeth rattling. I reached for my alarm clock, held it up to catch the slanting bit of light coming from the street-lamps. Three-twenty.

The wall was almost cold against my bare back, and I could feel the brush strokes that laid whiteness on the wall, the tiny canals pressed into the paint filling with my skin, wrinkling me. It was different than the cutting lines of weeds and sticks and twigs that seemed to push their way to my bones.

I pulled my knees up and lit a cigarette, moving slow as if my joints ached from the indecisive spring weather. It sounded frigid outside. Spring. It seems to take forever in showing up. When it does, I always spend days wishing it hadn't. I'd been lucky this season, too busy to think of spring. Too busy for the nightmare. Knew underneath it'd catch up, knew I'd soon spend nights awake, so awake I could hear things and feel things and see things that weren't for anybody else. I'd be cemented out of sleep, not allowed back till I chiseled out a new place to lay down. Will I spend nights and nights with this now? Will it be like the beginning, when it started, when Jessie would find me rigid and cold and sweating in my bed? By itself, I could deal with the dream. It was after.

I inhaled, my knuckles and the smoke lighting up orange. I was down to half a pack a week now, even when Cady helped smoke them. She'd only do it after we made love, when we shared one. I searched the floor for some clothes, finding a sweatshirt and a pair of jeans in a little heap.

The slush froze into chunks of ice shining orange by the streetlights and blue by the moon. My shoes slipped and skidded as I walked the four blocks over to her house. The back door was open — I knew because I'd been there the day Joe Don broke the lock and Cady tried to fix it — and I caught the screen before it could slam. I tiptoed across the kitchen and into the dining room. I could've gone up the back stairs, but they make so much noise I would've woke J.D. for sure. At least the front stairs were quiet.

I stepped into the living room.

A sharp snick and a flash of light. Flat to the wall I went, trying to disappear in the mural.

"Hi, dollface," Angel said in the light of her Bic, a cigarette hanging out the corner of her mouth. "Want to join me?" It went dark again.

The screaming under my skin stopped. I bobbed my head in the direction of the couch, then remembered she couldn't see me. "Yeah," I said gasping.

The tip of her cigarette glowed and faded. "Want to sit down?"

"No." Jesus. I lit a cigarette, my lungs getting a coating that was warm and thick and my eyes getting a new blue flash the same shape as the flame. "Where's the ashtray?"

"On the table, to your left."

I found it and dropped the match. Both cigarettes gleamed as we smoked in silence. She was waiting for me to explain, I could tell. I licked my wind-burned lips. "I'm sorry I surprised you," I started.

"You didn't," she said simply. The tip of her cigarette glowed.

"I was going to —"

"Why are you telling me? It's none of my business."

Somehow this didn't surprise me, I was dealing with Angel. I blew a smoke ring. Even in the dark I could tell it was perfect.

"Let me paint you, Amory," she spoke softly.

"No." My word carried smoke with it.

"Why not?"

"I don't want you to."

Her ember grew long and bright, then short again. "I could do it without you being there," she said.

"Go ahead then."

"No." I knew she was shaking her head. "No."

Cigarettes gleamed as we smoked in silence again. Too bad I can't breathe after smoking all day. I like the gray clouded feeling that seems to reach to my toes. It's always been that way, even when I first learned to smoke with Tara Maple in the woods by the junior high. Tara's daddy was the pastor of the church and she would smoke only with me because I knew how to keep my mouth shut and she figured I'd catch just as much hell if we were caught since Jess worked for the church, too. We would lean against the trees and she'd teach me to inhale, and when I could do that, she taught me all the tricks like blowing smoke out of my nose. Took me about a month to figure it all out without getting sick and I must've smoked half a pack in those first twenty minutes trying to learn it all.

"Let me photograph you."

The sound of her jerked me back to the living room. I rubbed my eyes. They felt bruised around the edges with the smoke and the lateness. I reached for the ashtray.

"Here it is."

"Thanks." Eyes used to the dark, I could see her outline framed in the window as I took it from her and crushed my cigarette out. "No."

"It'll only take an hour, Amory. You won't have to take all your clothes off."

"Take my clothes off?" I set the ashtray back on the table and stood up straight. "Who said I'd take my clothes off for anybody?"

"Just your shirt. I'll photograph you without your shirt."

"No, Angel, you will not photograph me without my shirt." Blood rushed into my legs, giving me goosebumps.

"Two rolls of film. We'll fight about your shirt later." I heard her shift, the leather jacket creaking with the way she moved and the tip of her cigarette glowed brightly once more.

* * * * *

"Cady?" I whispered. Nothing. "Cady?" I said again, a little louder.

She was flopped face down into her pillows, a sleeping lump. She turned over slowly and stretched. Then snapped frozen. "Who's it?"

"It's me."

"Amory?" Sleep shaken off for good. "You scared the shit out of me. What are you doing here?"

"I don't know." I stood still in the dark, watching her curve into grays on the bed across the room. It was stupid, running over here like this. "I just wanted to see you," I said, shuffling to get comfortable against the doorframe.

"My God." She lay back again. "I was having one of those funny dreams, when you keep waking up, you know. Then I saw somebody in my room."

"I'm sorry. I didn't mean to scare you." The wind knocked branches against branches and polished the last

169

of the snow to a high sheen that looked like drifting opals. "I really am."

"That's okay, hon. I'll be okay as long as I don't have a heart attack."

Pulling out a cigarette, I hunted in my pockets for a light. Damn. "Got any matches?"

"Sure." The sheets shifted with a papery sound. "They're over here."

I walked across the floor, slow measured steps that paced off the distance. "Where?"

"Right here."

I squatted down as a wooden match rasped. By the light of the flame, she didn't look like I'd just woken her up, her face wasn't heavy and lined from creases in the pillowcase or from her hair, but smooth. Her eyes shone the same green as satin Christmas ribbon.

I tapped the end of the cigarette. "Guess I don't need it anyway," I said, slipping it back.

"You want to talk?"

I shrugged in my jean jacket, feeling the heavy seams lining my skin. The flame sank and went out, leaving the smell of burnt wood hanging between us.

"You don't want to talk?"

"No," I whispered. I shut my eyes, seeing the gray shapes go darker than the blackness of the nightmare. The inside of my arms ached to feel how warm she was, how she could move and bend and twist. Remorse pricked at me like the wrong end of a wire brush. "Do you want me to go?"

"No," Cady said, reaching to touch my arm. "I want you to come." She was waking up more every second. "I thought you were mad at me."

I sat down cross-legged, losing her touch. "I am."

"Oh."

170

"It doesn't matter what happened, not anymore. I'm not mad now."

"I'm glad to hear that." Her fingers swept the bottom of my neck near my collarbone. "Cold out."

"Yes."

"Do you mind if I touch you here?" Cady said steadily.

"No. I don't mind." I could feel how warm she was through my shirt. My heart beat like a drum between my ears, causing my muscles to twang and my voice fall away to almost nothing.

Moving away, she sat up. "You don't want me to touch you?"

I picked up her hand and put it where it'd been, covering it with mine.

"I missed you," she whispered.

I dropped my head, aloneness sneaking up my back. Her fingers came up to rest on my cheek, touching the single tear that got away.

"What is it, baby?"

"Nothing, Cady. Nothing."

"Then will you get your clothes off and get into bed with me?"

Soon I was deep in the blankets, kissing her neck. I wanted to pull her into me, to feel the lines be crossed and uncrossed the same way we shifted legs and arms to fit each other. I wanted the hot flashing that made her shake and tremble and cry out as she arched and twisted and tightened. I ran my lips to where her collarbones arched and further where her breasts rose. Kissing her mouth, a fire lit itself between us and my hips rocked like flames move. A storm was breaking itself inside me, I could feel the blue-white streak of lightning behind my eyes and saw red-orange thunder as it exploded in my head. Her hand caught the back of my neck.

"Easy, baby, take it easy," Cady said, not sure where this was going. "We have all the time we need. I just woke up." She ran her hands through my hair.

I ducked my head back into her neck, tasting salt and smelling sleep. Our bodies slid from sweat.

Her hand clamped on my wrist. "Please stop."

"Stop?"

I fell back, a pounding in my shoulders and head that felt like my skin was twitching on the inside.

"What is going on? Tell me what's wrong." I could see her head silhouetted by the white ceiling as she leaned on her elbow.

"Nothing, Cady, I told you. Nothing's wrong. I just want you. Want you so much, I'm in a hurry."

"I don't believe you." She held my face in her hands as if to read my eyes by the gray moonlight.

I sighed, letting the hard bright fireworks in my head fade to softer colors.

"Come on," she said, "I'll rub your back."

I hesitated.

"Come on," she said again gently, "roll over."

Cady turned me onto my stomach, moving slow like I was a wild thing she didn't want to scare. I felt her nipples graze my back as she reached over to the small table. Straddling my hips as she had the first time, she sat up and began rubbing, her hands warm and slick from oil mixing with my sweat.

"Let go, my love, just let go," she said over and over, words and hazy light seeping in. I could see her form on the wall, her arms and hands moving, untying the hard black knots in my back. Sweet and slow and deep did she touch, the heat that had seared us sliding now into a warmth that spread and softened all the way to my fingertips. "Do you want to tell me, Ames?"

172

"Dream." My voice drowsy though I was awake. "The nightmare."

"Bad?"

"Bad."

She kept on massaging my legs and feet, kissing small places. Slowly the tightness unraveled with the sliding heat of her hands. Slower she touched, with the rhythm of a woman, every nerve ending, every fiber of me waiting, learning the pattern she would follow and change. The quiet heat built into a thin sheet of flame under my skin. She slipped her tongue up the middle of my back. I curled my fingers into fists, it felt so good. She lifted my shoulder and I turned over. The storm began again now in all of me, not breaking me as much as welding the shattered, frightened pieces with its steel as she kissed and brushed and touched. I rocked further, wanting the heat of her in every place. Her mouth slipped and slid, nipping my sides or my arms or my stomach. My fingers tied into her hair, uncurled, then tightened again.

I didn't feel her kissing the scar that divided me in two, just her breath wisping and her belly when she moved between my legs.

Colors pinwheel behind my eyelids. Small electric darts shoot up my back. Her tongue licks and tastes and the heat fills more than the room as she loves me and loves me and loves me.

* * * * *

"You taste good," she murmured against my ear as she lay on top of me.

My heart did another triple jump as I opened my eyes.

"You're beautiful." Her words tickled deep in my ear.

Cady, my lover.

173

She brushed hair out of my face. "I love to touch you."

"I think my bones melted."

She pulled the blankets over her back, covering us.

I closed my eyes to keep floating. "You are a wicked woman." We lay there so quiet I could hear the house grow old. "My god," I sighed with every part of me. I arched towards her, wanting her that close again. "I never —" I stopped, feeling a nasty tingle of embarrassment beginning behind my ears.

"You never what?"

My stomach hurt on all sides. "I never, uh, nobody ever, no one could ever, oh, hell."

"You never had an orgasm before."

I bit the inside of my cheek where it'd been healing. "Right."

"Oh." She nodded a little bit. "And you had one with me just now?"

I looked at the ceiling again. "Right."

"I'm glad."

I grinned. "Me too."

We both laughed.

"I asked somebody what it was like once," I said. Cady was brushing my skin with the ends of her fingers. "I never let on that I didn't know, you know? I asked her how she could tell if she'd had one and she said it was like getting your hand slammed in a car door. When it happens, you know it."

"Jesus."

"I'd take this over that any day."

"Me, too, hon. Me too." She sighed deep, happy. "Hey?"

"Yeah?"

"Would you like to maybe plan a weekend for just us?"

"When?" It was at least a month before school was out. I slipped my hands over her back, feeling her curves. Delicious.

"Next week?"

"I have a paper to write." It was going to be a bitch. I had it all planned how I was going to lock myself in my room with three cans of ravioli, all my research notes, and a bottle of rum.

"The weekend after? I'll make sure no one is here. We can be alone for three days."

"Okay. Yes. I'd like that."

"So would I." She kissed me.

"Can we sleep like this?"

"You wouldn't mind getting crushed by me lying on you all night?"

"I don't mind," I answered, holding her tighter around the waist.

"I love you, Amory."

Another triple jump by my heart. "I know that," I said, so soft I wasn't sure she heard till she giggled into my neck and we finally fell asleep.

* * * * *

"Look this way," Angel said a week later, touching my cheek. Pulling her hand away, I could feel where her fingers had touched, making a cold heat spin down my face that turned into color all the way to my feet. My nipples budded as she walked away.

Camera to her eye. "Are you cold?" Click, click, click, it went.

I crossed my arms. "You ever think of heating this place?"

Click, click, click.

"We'll move closer to the chimney in a minute. It's warmer over there."

Click, click, click.

"What do you want me to do now?"

"You're doing fine, Amory." Click, click, click, click. "Just fine."

A whistle shrilled all the way to the attic. I turned to the window looking for the kid making all the noise. There'd been five ten-year-olds on bikes this morning outside in the sun.

"Turn slowly back to me," Angel ordered. Click. Click. "Once more." Click, click, click, click. "Beautiful."

"Are you almost finished?"

Click, click, click.

"Pretty soon. This light is perfect."

Click, click.

The sun started feeling warm on my bare back and arms. I looked around the studio. Canvasses and sketches and piles of stones for sculptures were everywhere, even under her bed.

"Okay." Click. "Relax for a little while."

I got my shirt off the back of a chair and put it on. I liked this shirt. It was flannel and I bought it for a dollar at the army/navy store. It was cheap because one sleeve was longer than the other but with them rolled up who could tell the difference?

"Can you see the scar?"

"I can see it."

"Will it be in the pictures?"

"If I was into scars and freak shows, Amory, I'd kill myself and come back as the new Diane Arbus." She paused, setting the camera down and picking up a cigarette. "All right. I apologize. Again." A tiny snap from

176

Angel's lighter sounded in the attic. "I just wish you'd believe me when I say you have the perfect face."

I struck a match and lit up, too.

"Where did you get that, anyway?" she asked. "It's too messy for surgery, unless you had a shit-for-brains doctor, and too clean for a car wreck. Who knifed you?"

I grinned at her through the sunlight and the smoke. "Sometimes, Angel, you are a little too smart for your own damn good."

"People tell me that." She grinned back.

The sun pushed us into early afternoon. Every now and then a whistle would sound outside the window. I wandered the attic. Out the other window I could see through the budding trees and over the roof of the next house to Chase Stadium. But the canvasses around the window pulled me back into the room. Paintings stacked a foot deep to the wall, some six or seven feet wide, some little things the size of my hand, colors leaning against each other, parts of one against another turning them all into something else.

In a corner a sculpture curved, half covered by a cloth, next to it a mallet and some scarred pieces of metal. By the brick chimney, just out of the sun, another picture partly finished sat on an easel. I ashed my cigarette into a butt-filled cup on the stool, trying not to hit the tubes of paint and brushes lying there.

Angel's bed was on the other side of the chimney, a mess of unmade colors. Blankets, magazines, clothes, sketch pads took up any place to sleep. Two cartons of cigarettes were spilled open on the floor next to a comic book.

"When did you start smoking?"

She turned from the window and looked at me. "I start and stop. Goes in cycles. I get up to two packs a day then quit."

I stepped behind Angel to the top of the stairs, recognizing what was there for the first time. Tacked and taped and nailed were hundreds of sketches, pencil and charcoal and ink figures on every kind of paper: sketch pad, blue-lined notebook, paper bags, napkins — they filled the space between the small closet and the window. It was four feet of the same woman from every single view.

"Who is this?"

Angel got off the stool and started playing with her camera. "A dancer. She had a perfect body. We'd go to her studio and she'd dance naked in front of the mirrors and I'd sketch her for hours. Put out your cigarette. We have work to do."

* * * * *

Not able to sleep.

Cady's breathing is slow, saying her dreams are safe. Sleep is safe. I wonder.

Tonight we made love. We do most nights, most days even, but it was different this time. All evening her eyes danced with mine, making way, getting ready, each laugh touching skin. We came to her bed, clothing gone, and I found her as new and clean as the first time, the same breath-held excitement making my hands shake.

Cady kissed me again and again, spicing the softness with the quick slips of her tongue and biting my bottom lip. She brushed my belly and hip with her hand, kissing deeper in a new way. I curved toward her, bodies fit thigh

178

through thigh and breast to breast. Thick ribbons of heat from something more than the two of us made my skin tingle. Hot bands flashed colors against my squeezed-tight eyes, lacing us with carving, curving light.

I read in a book once about how women have a deep black triangle of self hidden away. Maybe these triangles crashed together and the braiding of light was the sparks of welding or collision.

* * * * *

I think I fell asleep around five. Cady kissed my back till I was awake and now watched me.

"Morning." Her voice was quiet and searching.

"Morning." I stared at the glass.

"Want some orange juice?"

I took the cup from her. It was a sports heroes glass from 7-11 with Martina Navratilova on it. The ink was flaking off, making her name look misspelled and her face blotchy.

I set the cup down and watched Cady. She was tracing an imaginary line from my knee to my thigh.

"Did you feel anything more than usual last night?"

"What do you mean?" She teased the inside of my leg.

"Stop that, it tickles. I don't know what I mean. It's hard to explain. Like something really big was wrapped around us like a pair of hands holding us together."

"Yes." She kissed my thigh.

"What was it?"

"God was here." She said it the same way a kid would explain how the universe was made.

"God? How do you figure that? I never heard of no god that did this kind of shit."

Stretching beside me, she threw one leg over mine and lay her hand across my belly over the scar. "God works in mysterious ways."

"My ass."

"That's right," she kissed, then nipped my neck, right near my collarbone.

"I am trying to have a discussion, Cady Baird, do you mind keeping your lips off me for a second?"

Cady sat up, sighed, and ruffled her red hair. "Be a lot easier if you stopped tempting me with your delicious and practically bare body."

I wrapped the sheet around me. "Okay?"

"Okay."

"Your hormones going to be all right?"

"Not if you keep stalling."

"All right already." I folded my hands in my lap. "So you do believe in god."

"Yes."

"Do you know there's a god?"

"As far as knowing can take me," she replied.

I pulled her on top of me. Hugging hard, I wanted her to sink through to my skin. "You're groovy."

"You're just saying that because I wear a D-cup. Are we finished talking?"

"For now." I hugged her again.

She started humming. "Crazy." "Want to dance?"

"Huh?"

"Dance. You know. What we do at night but standing up."

"I have to go to the can, Cady."

"Get up, come on," she insisted, pulling me out of bed. Floorboards creaking, we slowly spun naked and warm, around and around.

"You better let me go or I'm going to spring a leak."

"So what?" She started singing away and we both giggled nose to nose till the song ended. "I like the way Linda Ronstadt sings it best."

"Better than Patsy Kline? Girl, your head needs fixed. Now let me go."

"What was Jessie like?"

"We're done talking for now, remember?"

"I'm serious."

"You'll do anything to keep me hanging around." I dropped my hands to the small of her back, both touching fingertip to fingertip, and shrugged. "She was just Jessie." Her hair was soft as I twirled it in my hand.

"How?"

"She had her way of doing things. When she got older she thought it was the only way of doing things. It happens to everybody, far as I can see."

"Not my parents. Sometimes I even think we're having a contest to see who can be more radical." She traced the line of my jaw. "What did she look like?"

"Her hair was short, a little further past her ears and parted on the side. She wasn't very tall and got a little heavy on the hoof when she started drinking."

"She drank a lot?"

"I don't know if it was a lot, but she drank. And she always wore dresses and sensible shoes and in the winter she'd add white sweaters with fake pearl buttons."

"Did you cry when she died?"

I shook my head. "Never seemed to be a reason. She thought there was a heaven and believed she was going. I guess she's better off now than when she was alive."

Her fingers rested on my collarbones. "Did you like her?"

"Like her? I don't know. We got along till I went wild. Got to be where we couldn't be in the same room together without fighting like cats."

"Did you love her?"

Love. I got to think about that. "I guess so. Yeah, I think I did. Maybe I still do, but so much of Jess got caught up in her own god stuff, seemed she didn't have time for me. Especially after this." I touched the long scar down my belly. "Baptists are a little strange, always thinking that bad things happen to bad people, not that bad people do bad things. Jackie was the worst human being imaginable and Jessie laid the whole thing on my back as if I was to blame."

"You didn't believe it?"

"Took me awhile to start disbelieving." I shrugged. "I was raised a Baptist, thinking I had to hide things, be ashamed, believe it was my fault. Hard to break a habit of a lifetime and stop hiding what's hardest to bear. I don't think Jess ever learned to stop hiding things, about her, about me, about the bottles she hid in the china hutch."

"You found those."

"Of course. The only thing I ever uncovered."

"So far." She smiled.

I smiled back. "So far." Damn, she was a beautiful woman. "Now, will you let me go to the bathroom?"

"Was Jessie cute?"

"When she was younger. I saw a picture."

"Was she cute as me?"

"No one's cute as you, Cady Baird."

"Damn right." She lay her head on my shoulder.

"Found an old scrapbook she'd hid away. Lots of pictures of me in it, and that one of her, too, if you want to see them."

"I'd like that," she said, suddenly biting my neck again, then kissing me.

* * * * *

The evening was still warm. Me and Cady and this whole weekend. We could lie in the sun or go to Juniper's or stay in bed as long as we wanted. I threw my backpack, lumpy because Jessie's photo album was too big to fit right, in the jeep. Noticing all the trash littering the floor, I grabbed a McDonald's bag and started cleaning, filling it with pop cans and papers and cigarette butts that had been lying around for god knows how long, and crumpled it all together.

The full bag went into Cady's neighbors' garbage can sitting at the edge of the grass. Angel's Triumph sat in the driveway, nose out in case she had to make a quick getaway.

I walked into the house, shouting for Cady. "Hi, sweetheart!" I tossed my backpack into a chair and spun her around, kissing and laughing. "I brought clothes so I won't have to go back unless we have a big fight."

Her eyes were shiny and she kissed me back. "I love you, Amory."

"You best be careful, Cady Baird. Every word you say flies off into infinity and some day they'll all come back to bear witness against you."

"I love you," she said again. I pulled her tight, feeling how well we fit. She put her hands to my face. This is a good thing, I could almost hear her thinking, this is a good thing.

"Angel has the pictures," she said, still holding on. "They're incredible. She really sees you, Ames. She

183

promised to give me one." Cady kissed me short and quick. "They're beautiful."

"We'll look at them later, okay?"

"Okay."

I kissed her this time, tasting her mouth.

"How about some dinner and then we decide what we want to do next?"

"I know exactly what I want to do next," I answered.

* * * * *

The house was quiet and we lay on the floor of her room, the dark sliding away from us like a thick blanket.

Watching Cady sleep. Watching the sharp right-angles of her shoulder blades, like little wings. Soft, sleek curve of her back and arching hip a perfect one-third circle, not like the flat-topped bone of mine. In the uncurling light of sunrise, waves of ribs rolled to her breasts. Her right one is bigger than the left, we compared. Daniel had been right; she has quite a set.

Cady's brother Duncan sent her a letter. I couldn't read it because the kid can't write, I mean he's physically barely able to, even though he's thirteen years old. She was so proud of him; he typed her address onto the envelope with x's around the outside. I guess he loves her as much as she loves him.

She stretched and moaned, her voice low pitched like a tree when the wind pesters only the topmost branches, bending them enough to make the trunk shift.

I pinched my nipples, rolling them between my fingers. Not much there really. It'd bugged Daniel, me not being stacked, though he never said much about it. It bugged most of the guys, but never to a point where they quit what they were doing. Cady doesn't mind, she said so and I believe her, she said she likes me like this. Said she loves me like this.

Maybe that's why she touches and kisses so I can feel it and don't want her to stop.

Maybe if I stare at her long enough she'll wake up.

* * * * *

I walked out to the kitchen combing my hair back. The water rolled onto my sweatshirt, leaving dark marks that grew warm from the heat of my body and the morning sun. A cup of coffee waited on the table with a pack of cigarettes and an ashtray. Cady was leaning back in her chair, eyes half open.

"You look like you just got out of bed." My voice was low and quiet as I bent down.

She moaned as our mouths touched, kissing like she was hungry for me all over again. "What time is it?"

"About ten." I sat down. She took my breath away just sitting there.

"Do you want to see the photographs?"

"Sure," I said, not so sure. I put the comb on the table and lit a cigarette.

Cady was back in a second, carrying a stack big enough to need two hands. She sifted through them and sat down. "I like this one and this one the best."

"Then just give me those."

She set them in front of me. I put my cigarette out and rolled my eyes. Terrific. The first one was black and white and I was standing near the window, arms crossed, the light shining on my face and shoulder and the round part of my belly near where my jeans started. The scar was almost lost in the silvery grain, but I could see it. I could always see it.

"Aren't they unbelievable?"

I dropped that one and picked up the next. It was closer, a picture of my face and neck, collarbones neatly framed by my right thumb and forefinger. I was looking into the camera, black next to the white that lit my face.

My face.

"Ames?"

I've seen this before.

"Amory?"

It seemed to jump as I watched. This face. These eyes. A picture of me. But I've seen it before.

"Amory!"

I ran upstairs and dumped my backpack, the album spinning out, falling with its pages spread against the floor. I picked it up, turned to the second page. The girls, Jessie, Sylvia, and the other one, Joanna Nobody, the one that haunts when my poems are good.

"What is it? What's wrong?" Cady asked, hand on my shoulder.

My eyes shine out of a photograph older than I am.

"Let me see it, Ames." The book shifted as she looked.

Her. That's her. Oh, god, with a face younger than mine.

"Joanna Nobody."

"Who?" Cady took the picture out of my hand and studied it. "Joanna who?"

The album sat in my lap. I stared at Jessie's face, bright and clear and smiling. Jess and Joanna. "My ghost," I whispered. Jess never told me. She never told me.

"My god, Amory." Cady stared. "Your faces are exactly the same."

I shoved my clothes back in the pack and stood up.

"Wait!" she shouted down the stairs.

I threw my backpack into the jeep. The morning sun scattered its way through the leaves to the street, making everything shift in the wind.

"Where are you going?" She was breathing hard.

"I'm going back. Tell McClure." I got in as she watched me. Her eyes got less and less filled with fire and more and more like snow frozen by the wind. "Tell McClure I'll be back. No. Tell her I'll call. No," I shook my head again, trying to get what I meant right in my own mind. "Tell her, tell her whatever you want."

"Where are you going?"

"To find Sylvia. To find Joanna Nobody. I already know Jessie's burning in hell."

She caught my hand. "You don't have to go."

"Yes, Cady." The words blazed out. "Yes. Yes I do."

"Why?" she demanded. "Why? None of it means anything anymore, you said so yourself."

"It does now." I looked at her standing there, shoulder to the roll bar, hands fisted at her waist and holding on very, very tight, eyes getting brittle with cold. Cady Baird became tiny in the silver spring light.

"It has nothing to do with you, baby. Nothing. Please," I spoke quiet and soft as the wind, "please let me go."

Cady spun away, muscles tight enough to rise out the back of her shirt as she paced, peering into the jeep.

"I have to." The words barely carried.

"You don't." She looked steady at me, putting more into her look so's for me to catch.

I gritted my teeth. How much I want what's here right now. How much I wanted these three unbroken days, days we haven't shared since that sunlit cold time months ago. Time. Time was stepping on itself in order to get by me, confusing everything till minutes that followed one by

187

one seemed unconnected. If this had come with Daniel, leaving would have been nothing, as brief as the last shadows before I blew out a candle, as meaningful as anonymous traffic that passes outside a window.

"Jessie would understand."

Jessie? "Jess understand? Never was a question of Jessie understanding." I stared down the quiet street. "It was always her circus she was running, her giving orders, her keeping secrets, her knowing all." I slammed my hands against the wheel. The pain felt good. "She never told me a thing, Cady. Jess never told me a thing."

Cady's eyes went liquid green, the color emeralds are supposed to be but never are. "But you have a new life here. With me."

"Can't have a new life till I finish with the old one."

"Stay, Amory. Please."

I tried to smile, tried so hard I had to shut my own eyes in the face of the lie. "I believe, Cady Baird, that you would ask me to marry you if such things were legal."

"Don't Ames. Don't tease. Don't you know I'd give you the answers to this if I could?" She stared at the ground. "Do you want me to come with you?"

"No," I answered softly.

"I didn't think you would." Cady reached out to touch my face, brushing gently. "Call me," she said, dropping her hand and stepping back away. "Write. Anything. Be careful. I love you."

I slammed the door shut. Driving down the street, I glanced in the mirror. Her body turned to a speck against the glass then disappeared.

* * * * *

It used to be green out here. Really green. Jess and I would come out here when I was little. Used to be just the West Virginia woods and the gray band of road coming through, with only the river and the forest between here and Sterling. Till somebody big enough wanted more wood and more land to throw the slag from the mines onto. No trees now, just stumps on the ridge sticking out like rotting teeth.

I lit a cigarette and downshifted, turning towards town. Same strip of two-lane with billboards every half mile. I haven't been back for three years and all they managed to do was chop down more trees. After two puffs I shoved the cigarette out where a snap had busted off the soft top.

My eyes felt full of sand after nineteen hours of no sleep and non-stop freeway. I tried talking to Jess, to practice what I was going to say but got no answer. Spirits can't cross moving water and I was dead sure as soon as I crossed the Suicide Bridge she was going to show up in the seat next to me, waiting for another fight.

I held my breath and crossed the bridge into downtown. Nothing. Market Street was the same. The courthouse was deserted and the statue of Tecumseh gray as ever. Poor guy, having to stand out there night and day letting the birds shit all over his shirt. They got the name for the high school team from Tecumseh. The Sterling Wild Indians. Should be the Sterling Silver Assholes for all the good it did them.

Daniel's bookstore was now Ford's Illumination Company, We'll Light up Your Life, a handpainted sign said in the window. The shades were pulled and a soggy U.S. flag hung by the pole to the right of the door. Christ.

I parked the jeep and got out, lighting another cigarette. Jake's was still standing. It'll always be standing. After a nuclear war, the cockroaches and gonorrhea will have a place to hang out at Jake's Bar and Grill.

Back now. In a town that means having no future, just a past everyone else knows but me. A place can't tell stories. A town can't give dreams. It's just the crossroads of disappointment and failure built on ground hollowed out and emptied by desperate people. I can feel the tunnels underneath. Maybe I was born with a caul that made me magic. More like I was born feet first and been backasswards ever since.

I looked both ways and crossed the street.

Stepping through the door, I scanned the empty place. A new moosehead hung on the wall. That was a shocker, never heard of a moose traveling this far, especially not with a cigarette hanging out its lips.

"Sit yourself down." Her voice came from the back. "Be with youse in a minute."

I sat at the table by the door and she waddled over. Sylvia. In the same white uniform. "What can I get you?" she asked, only to stop three feet from the table. She recognized me even in the shadows.

"I could use a beer."

She brought a glass and a cardboard coaster with a Budweiser logo on it.

"Thanks." I took a swallow. "Oh, don't leave, Sylvia. Why don't you sit down for a while? I'd like to talk with you."

"What would you have to say to me?"

I studied her, beehive hairdo and footsore walk and yellow-white skin from being inside all the time. "Sit down. You know what it's about."

"What do you want?" she asked, hands denting the fat at her hips.

"Jessie Walker died before telling me things I have a right to know."

"So you come expecting me to?"

I nodded my yes. "Come on." I pulled the table closer to me to make room for her on the other side.

"You are mighty mistaken if you think I owe you something."

"You don't owe me, Sylvia. I just want the truth." I drank some beer, feeling every touch of coldness in my throat. "Why don't you start at the beginning?"

"Why should I tell you anything, Miss Amy Walker?"

I shrugged, pretending I didn't want to grab her by the jowls and throw her into the seat. "I figure I still know enough people willing to tell me about Jess and Joanna."

Her jaw moved a little sideways and she tilted her chin up. For a second she looked like a shrewd pig, her eyes shining like marbles.

"I know her name. I know enough to start asking questions, get people blabbering."

"It's all over and done with. What do you want?"

Maybe it's done for you, Sylvia. "That's my business."

"You don't think the Macons are going to give you anything, do you?"

Macons? What the hell do they have to do with this? "Can't count on them for nothing but lies. I'm looking for some answers."

"They won't give you nothing, no matter what you try. Didn't give me nothing, didn't give Joannie nothing."

"Did they owe her?"

"They didn't. David Macon did. Still does, if you ask me."

"David Macon?" I tilted my head toward the booth. She swung her bulk around and sat down.

"David Macon. The one who lives in the great big house and sends his kids to college and goes wherever he wants whenever he wants. We was going to get married, till she laid her eyes on him."

"Who? Jess?"

"Joanna. She always was the grabby type."

"Oh, yeah?" I arched my eyebrow.

"Don't be thinking you can use that tone of voice with me, little girl. You wanted to know and I'm telling you. Start acting like that and I'll get back to what I was doing. I'm running a business here, you know."

I bit my tongue, then drank some more beer to keep quiet.

"She was grabby, always looking for an easy way out, thought she found it with David Macon." She scraped some dried crap off the tabletop, brushing away the shavings. "He was a good-looking man then. You look like your mama, except your hair. That's his, curly and thick and black."

I ran my fingers through my father's hair. David Macon. Jessie never even told me this much.

"You got her smile. And you got her way of looking down on things. More than anything she wanted out of here, thought being educated would do it. Spent most her time in the library, till she caught sight of my man."

David Macon. That would make me a Macon, too. I started to sweat. Jessie never said anything and now it's all tumbling out like lava.

"She got pregnant, Joannie did. Thought she had him for sure. But he left, stayed away from Sterling for three years. She finally packed up and went to Philadelphia, Jess following like a basset hound. All alone they went,

Joanna to have you and Jessie to pay the bills. Don't know why they picked Philadelphia, guess they had nowhere else to go since neither one had family left. I did hear that Joannie had a brother once who lived south. Hanged himself in some jail or other."

I squeezed my eyes shut. A bead of sweat slid past my temple. For a flash, I could see Jessie's coffin after the funeral, the dates on the marker buried under dirt.

"Jess always wrote me letters. She was a great one for that. She even talked Joanna into sending me a card telling me about you. I think Joannie would've liked to keep it quiet, though you can't keep a secret like that around here for long, but Jess was proud of you. October fourteenth it said on this little card with your name on it. Amory." She spat it out like it tasted bad. "Some strange name she found in some strange book."

"This Side of Paradise."

"What did you say, girl? Get your fingers out of your mouth."

"This Side of Paradise. It's a novel."

"Just like her," Sylvia snorted. "Always flaunting her brains."

I drank the last of the beer but it didn't wash the dryness out of my throat. "Where is she now?" I managed to get out.

"Joanna? She's dead. Died right after you were born." Sylvia leaned forward, the reflection on the formica making her seem twice as big. "I think maybe she took her own life, wouldn't've surprised me though no one ever said, least of all Jessie Walker. Joanna never was one for hardships."

"And you are?"

"I got this far, didn't I? All by myself with no help from anybody. I done all right."

"Yeah, you done all right." I emptied my glass and shoved it and the coaster to the edge of the table.

"Another?"

I shook my head and lit a cigarette, wanting my own private fog of smoke. "What then, Sylvia?"

She lifted her hands like a pastor ready to give a blessing and rolled her massive shoulders. "Jess came back alone, set up that adoption through the church like we all didn't know whose you were. But we're all taught to keep our noses out of bad people's business. David Macon came back a year or two later, married to that New York bitch who left him after their freak Jackie was locked up in the Straitsville nuthouse after what happened to you. I wouldn't've left him, ever. I would've made David Macon happy, you bet I would have."

"Sure. Sure, I believe you." A cobweb of sadness floated across me. "You always hated me, Sylvia. Was this why? Is this all there is to it?"

She sat back in the booth and stared at me for a second. "Hate you? No. I never hated you." She got up from the table, moving pretty fast for a woman her size. "To me, honey, you never was alive."

* * * * *

Two hundred feet past the City Limits sign, before the land was split by barbed wire and No Trespassing signs, the graveyard stretched on with stone after stone standing at attention across the thick green grass. I lit a cigarette, its taste filling my mouth with ashes. Two more puffs and I dropped it into the grass, crushing it dead under my heel.

"There you go, Jess. For your edification," I said out loud, the only sound since the cemetery was quiet like it was supposed to be.

Way by the fence, mausoleums with Greek columns lurched out of the ground like new molars. Macons buried there. Her marker was simple, the dates clear this time. To anybody walking by this spot of earth, Jessie C. Walker had definitely lived and died — death had mailed her away and this was the postage stamp. Nothing big for her, no big white polished crypt shining in the sun. Not her style.

"Jessie, why didn't you tell me?" I whispered. "Did you love her Jessie? Did you hate him? What was she like, Jess, was she beautiful?"

My hands ached, fisted so tight in my pockets. She'd been gray-yellow, the skin of her face like old worn silk so transparent I could see her bones at the visitation. The coffin had been open and she lay there in her new burgundy dress and I swear any second her eyes were going to peel back and she was going to yell at me one last time before they had a chance to close the lid. But nothing happened. Jess kept quiet and still.

Always. "So fucking silent. What was it Jessie, that kept you so quiet even when I was begging for any drop of knowing them? Did people talk, Jess, about how you followed that woman, cried for her, raised her child, all out of love? Did they point at you and laugh and call us all bad names?"

The edges of white-barked trees seemed to burn like Moses' bush. I didn't ask for any of this, Jessie Walker. I never wanted to be a picture on the wall, a sign of someone else's sin.

Wild anger clawed through my arms and legs, shoving the ache in my muscles out of the way. "Did you try to look at me the same way Mary in the Bible did, trying to keep everything that mattered in your heart till nothing could fit anymore? Did loving me give you too much grief? There were things I had a right to know. Why didn't you say who they were, the ones that made me? Was I made in love? In hate? In the backseat of a Chevy with a bottle of tequila? And Jackie —" A Macon. Another one. The anger fell away like lamplight overpowered by the sun, my eyes growing clear.

"You used to say death came in threes, Jess. The first was Joanna's. The second was you." Sun lit tiny rainbows on my lashes till daylight was red against my eyes. A soft breeze was enough to start me swaying, I felt so tired. "It's me, isn't it, Jessie? I'm third. I died to you long before they put you in the ground. Dead since that day, the day you found me naked and bleeding in that field because of my brother. My brother. Wasn't that it? Didn't you start thinking me dead then, Jessie? The worst had been done to the daughter of a sinner. Not Joanna the sinner — you. Not Joanna's daughter, but your daughter and hers — me. You were in love, Jessie. Wasn't that the sin that made you look at me as a whip across your back?"

I inhaled, eyes aching and air catching the swelling in my throat to sound like a sigh. "Was I nothing to you but a punishment? You let me go, let me think I had no past, leaving me no way to begin. How could you give me up so easy, without even a fight?"

* * * * *

I can't make a rope out of sand, Jessie, and that's all you gave me.

196

Walking halfway down the bridge, I could still hear the keys jangling in the ignition from the wind blowing. So early in spring yet heat ghosts rose off the road, shimmering and dancing till I got to where they'd been standing and they'd move further away as I tightrope-walked the straight slashes of yellow that split the bridge in two.

Never had the chance to set it right, every time I asked, Jess, I'd get smacked across the mouth like I'd said a dirty word. You never set it true, what was left for me to believe in?

I turned sharp and walked to the railing. The water was the same cold gray cutting through the hills. My last cigarette I took out of the pack, the wind took it, slipping and spinning its way to the water. The river didn't notice, just kept flowing past other coal towns built on mines and mills and the greed of men like David Macon.

My father.

I leaned over as the river rushed by. The ground ain't solid nowhere, Jessie, and that's a fact. All the simplicity and words in the world can't begin to fill what's empty. You never said a thing, Jess, but even silence can speak.

The wind in the trees rustled, sounding like a crowd of strangers whispering secrets. What now? West towards the land of spaghetti westerns? North to the big cities, New York, Boston, that can eat a woman up like a machine? South to the evil that rides underneath the scrubbed whiteness and good manners like a sewer beneath a church? Back to Cady who wants to be everything for me when I don't even know what that is?

The wind paused for breath and I lit up. I threw the burnt match over, leaning against the rail to watch it fall as long as I could. It was so small it didn't even make a splash. How cold would the water be against skin?

Does the water cave in looking from underneath?
Does it hurt to hit it from this high up?

I leaned further over, far enough to see the shadow of the bridge on the water. You never told me, you never said, Jessie, and you left me without knowing what was mine to know.

Flicking the cigarette, I watched it arc up then down in slow motion against the too blue sky. Its curve was delicate as a ballet. My boots scraped, making a sound like sandpaper against my teeth as I spun to leave the river cutting steel through the earth.

A few of the publications of
THE NAIAD PRESS, INC.
P.O. Box 10543 ● Tallahassee, Florida 32302
Phone (904) 539-9322
Mail orders welcome. Please include 15% postage.

THE FINER GRAIN by Denise Ohio. 216 pp. Brilliant young
college lesbian novel.   ISBN 0-941483-11-8 $8.95

THE AMAZON TRAIL by Lee Lynch. 216 pp. Life, travel & lore
of famous lesbian author.   ISBN 0-941483-27-4   8.95

HIGH CONTRAST by Jessie Lattimore. 264 pp. Women of the
Crystal Palace.   ISBN 0-941483-17-7   8.95

OCTOBER OBSESSION by Meredith More. Josie's rich, secret
Lesbian life.   ISBN 0-941483-18-5   8.95

LESBIAN CROSSROADS by Ruth Baetz. 276 pp. Contemporary
Lesbian lives.   ISBN 0-941483-21-5   9.95

BEFORE STONEWALL: THE MAKING OF A GAY AND
LESBIAN COMMUNITY by Andrea Weiss & Greta Schiller.
96 pp., 25 illus.   ISBN 0-941483-20-7   7.95

WE WALK THE BACK OF THE TIGER by Patricia A. Murphy.
192 pp. Romantic Lesbian novel/beginning women's movement.
                                         ISBN 0-941483-13-4   8.95

SUNDAY'S CHILD by Joyce Bright. 216 pp. Lesbian athletics, at
last the novel about sports.   ISBN 0-941483-12-6   8.95

OSTEN'S BAY by Zenobia N. Vole. 204 pp. Sizzling adventure
romance set on Bonaire.   ISBN 0-941483-15-0   8.95

LESSONS IN MURDER by Claire McNab. 216 pp. 1st in a stylish
mystery series.   ISBN 0-941483-14-2   8.95

YELLOWTHROAT by Penny Hayes. 240 pp. Margarita, bandit,
kidnaps Julia.   ISBN 0-941483-10-X   8.95

SAPPHISTRY: THE BOOK OF LESBIAN SEXUALITY by
Pat Califia. 3d edition, revised. 208 pp.   ISBN 0-941483-24-X   8.95

CHERISHED LOVE by Evelyn Kennedy. 192 pp. Erotic
Lesbian love story.   ISBN 0-941483-08-8   8.95

LAST SEPTEMBER by Helen R. Hull. 208 pp. Six stories & a
glorious novella.   ISBN 0-941483-09-6   8.95

THE SECRET IN THE BIRD by Camarin Grae. 312 pp. Striking,
psychological suspense novel.   ISBN 0-941483-05-3   8.95

TO THE LIGHTNING by Catherine Ennis. 208 pp. Romantic
Lesbian 'Robinson Crusoe' adventure.   ISBN 0-941483-06-1   8.95

THE OTHER SIDE OF VENUS by Shirley Verel. 224 pp.
Luminous, romantic love story. ISBN 0-941483-07-X 8.95

DREAMS AND SWORDS by Katherine V. Forrest. 192 pp.
Romantic, erotic, imaginative stories. ISBN 0-941483-03-7 8.95

MEMORY BOARD by Jane Rule. 336 pp. Memorable novel
about an aging Lesbian couple. ISBN 0-941483-02-9 8.95

THE ALWAYS ANONYMOUS BEAST by Lauren Wright
Douglas. 224 pp. A Caitlin Reese mystery. First in a series.
ISBN 0-941483-04-5 8.95

SEARCHING FOR SPRING by Patricia A. Murphy. 224 pp.
Novel about the recovery of love. ISBN 0-941483-00-2 8.95

DUSTY'S QUEEN OF HEARTS DINER by Lee Lynch. 240 pp.
Romantic blue-collar novel. ISBN 0-941483-01-0 8.95

PARENTS MATTER by Ann Muller. 240 pp. Parents'
relationships with Lesbian daughters and gay sons.
ISBN 0-930044-91-6 9.95

THE PEARLS by Shelley Smith. 176 pp. Passion and fun in
the Caribbean sun. ISBN 0-930044-93-2 7.95

MAGDALENA by Sarah Aldridge. 352 pp. Epic Lesbian novel
set on three continents. ISBN 0-930044-99-1 8.95

THE BLACK AND WHITE OF IT by Ann Allen Shockley.
144 pp. Short stories. ISBN 0-930044-96-7 7.95

SAY JESUS AND COME TO ME by Ann Allen Shockley. 288
pp. Contemporary romance. ISBN 0-930044-98-3 8.95

LOVING HER by Ann Allen Shockley. 192 pp. Romantic love
story. ISBN 0-930044-97-5 7.95

MURDER AT THE NIGHTWOOD BAR by Katherine V.
Forrest. 240 pp. A Kate Delafield mystery. Second in a series.
ISBN 0-930044-92-4 8.95

ZOE'S BOOK by Gail Pass. 224 pp. Passionate, obsessive love
story. ISBN 0-930044-95-9 7.95

WINGED DANCER by Camarin Grae. 228 pp. Erotic Lesbian
adventure story. ISBN 0-930044-88-6 8.95

PAZ by Camarin Grae. 336 pp. Romantic Lesbian adventurer
with the power to change the world. ISBN 0-930044-89-4 8.95

SOUL SNATCHER by Camarin Grae. 224 pp. A puzzle, an
adventure, a mystery — Lesbian romance. ISBN 0-930044-90-8 8.95

THE LOVE OF GOOD WOMEN by Isabel Miller. 224 pp.
Long-awaited new novel by the author of the beloved *Patience
and Sarah.* ISBN 0-930044-81-9 8.95

THE HOUSE AT PELHAM FALLS by Brenda Weathers. 240
pp. Suspenseful Lesbian ghost story. ISBN 0-930044-79-7 7.95

HOME IN YOUR HANDS by Lee Lynch. 240 pp. More stories
from the author of *Old Dyke Tales.*   ISBN 0-930044-80-0   7.95

EACH HAND A MAP by Anita Skeen. 112 pp. Real-life poems
that touch us all.   ISBN 0-930044-82-7   6.95

SURPLUS by Sylvia Stevenson. 342 pp. A classic early Lesbian
novel.   ISBN 0-930044-78-9   7.95

PEMBROKE PARK by Michelle Martin. 256 pp. Derring-do
and daring romance in Regency England.   ISBN 0-930044-77-0   7.95

THE LONG TRAIL by Penny Hayes. 248 pp. Vivid adventures
of two women in love in the old west.   ISBN 0-930044-76-2   8.95

HORIZON OF THE HEART by Shelley Smith. 192 pp. Hot
romance in summertime New England.   ISBN 0-930044-75-4   7.95

AN EMERGENCE OF GREEN by Katherine V. Forrest. 288
pp. Powerful novel of sexual discovery.   ISBN 0-930044-69-X   8.95

THE LESBIAN PERIODICALS INDEX edited by Claire
Potter. 432 pp. Author & subject index.   ISBN 0-930044-74-6   29.95

DESERT OF THE HEART by Jane Rule. 224 pp. A classic;
basis for the movie *Desert Hearts.*   ISBN 0-930044-73-8   7.95

SPRING FORWARD/FALL BACK by Sheila Ortiz Taylor.
288 pp. Literary novel of timeless love.   ISBN 0-930044-70-3   7.95

FOR KEEPS by Elisabeth Nonas. 144 pp. Contemporary novel
about losing and finding love.   ISBN 0-930044-71-1   7.95

TORCHLIGHT TO VALHALLA by Gale Wilhelm. 128 pp.
Classic novel by a great Lesbian writer.   ISBN 0-930044-68-1   7.95

LESBIAN NUNS: BREAKING SILENCE edited by Rosemary
Curb and Nancy Manahan. 432 pp. Unprecedented autobiographies
of religious life.   ISBN 0-930044-62-2   9.95

THE SWASHBUCKLER by Lee Lynch. 288 pp. Colorful novel
set in Greenwich Village in the sixties.   ISBN 0-930044-66-5   8.95

MISFORTUNE'S FRIEND by Sarah Aldridge. 320 pp. Histori-
cal Lesbian novel set on two continents.   ISBN 0-930044-67-3   7.95

A STUDIO OF ONE'S OWN by Ann Stokes. Edited by
Dolores Klaich. 128 pp. Autobiography.   ISBN 0-930044-64-9   7.95

SEX VARIANT WOMEN IN LITERATURE by Jeannette
Howard Foster. 448 pp. Literary history.   ISBN 0-930044-65-7   8.95

A HOT-EYED MODERATE by Jane Rule. 252 pp. Hard-hitting
essays on gay life; writing; art.   ISBN 0-930044-57-6   7.95

INLAND PASSAGE AND OTHER STORIES by Jane Rule.
288 pp. Wide-ranging new collection.   ISBN 0-930044-56-8   7.95

WE TOO ARE DRIFTING by Gale Wilhelm. 128 pp. Timeless
Lesbian novel, a masterpiece.   ISBN 0-930044-61-4   6.95

AMATEUR CITY by Katherine V. Forrest. 224 pp. A Kate Delafield mystery. First in a series. ISBN 0-930044-55-X   7.95

THE SOPHIE HOROWITZ STORY by Sarah Schulman. 176 pp. Engaging novel of madcap intrigue. ISBN 0-930044-54-1   7.95

THE BURNTON WIDOWS by Vickie P. McConnell. 272 pp. A Nyla Wade mystery, second in the series. ISBN 0-930044-52-5   7.95

OLD DYKE TALES by Lee Lynch. 224 pp. Extraordinary stories of our diverse Lesbian lives. ISBN 0-930044-51-7   8.95

DAUGHTERS OF A CORAL DAWN by Katherine V. Forrest. 240 pp. Novel set in a Lesbian new world. ISBN 0-930044-50-9   7.95

THE PRICE OF SALT by Claire Morgan. 288 pp. A milestone novel, a beloved classic. ISBN 0-930044-49-5   8.95

AGAINST THE SEASON by Jane Rule. 224 pp. Luminous, complex novel of interrelationships. ISBN 0-930044-48-7   8.95

LOVERS IN THE PRESENT AFTERNOON by Kathleen Fleming. 288 pp. A novel about recovery and growth. ISBN 0-930044-46-0   8.95

TOOTHPICK HOUSE by Lee Lynch. 264 pp. Love between two Lesbians of different classes. ISBN 0-930044-45-2   7.95

MADAME AURORA by Sarah Aldridge. 256 pp. Historical novel featuring a charismatic "seer." ISBN 0-930044-44-4   7.95

CURIOUS WINE by Katherine V. Forrest. 176 pp. Passionate Lesbian love story, a best-seller. ISBN 0-930044-43-6   8.95

BLACK LESBIAN IN WHITE AMERICA by Anita Cornwell. 141 pp. Stories, essays, autobiography. ISBN 0-930044-41-X   7.50

CONTRACT WITH THE WORLD by Jane Rule. 340 pp. Powerful, panoramic novel of gay life. ISBN 0-930044-28-2   7.95

YANTRAS OF WOMANLOVE by Tee A. Corinne. 64 pp. Photos by noted Lesbian photographer. ISBN 0-930044-30-4   6.95

MRS. PORTER'S LETTER by Vicki P. McConnell. 224 pp. The first Nyla Wade mystery. ISBN 0-930044-29-0   7.95

TO THE CLEVELAND STATION by Carol Anne Douglas. 192 pp. Interracial Lesbian love story. ISBN 0-930044-27-4   6.95

THE NESTING PLACE by Sarah Aldridge. 224 pp. A three-woman triangle—love conquers all! ISBN 0-930044-26-6   7.95

THIS IS NOT FOR YOU by Jane Rule. 284 pp. A letter to a beloved is also an intricate novel. ISBN 0-930044-25-8   8.95

FAULTLINE by Sheila Ortiz Taylor. 140 pp. Warm, funny, literate story of a startling family. ISBN 0-930044-24-X   6.95

THE LESBIAN IN LITERATURE by Barbara Grier. 3d ed. Foreword by Maida Tilchen. 240 pp. Comprehensive bibliography. Literary ratings; rare photos. ISBN 0-930044-23-1   7.95

ANNA'S COUNTRY by Elizabeth Lang. 208 pp. A woman
finds her Lesbian identity.   ISBN 0-930044-19-3   6.95

PRISM by Valerie Taylor. 158 pp. A love affair between two
women in their sixties.   ISBN 0-930044-18-5   6.95

BLACK LESBIANS: AN ANNOTATED BIBLIOGRAPHY
compiled by J. R. Roberts. Foreword by Barbara Smith. 112 pp.
Award-winning bibliography.   ISBN 0-930044-21-5   5.95

THE MARQUISE AND THE NOVICE by Victoria Ramstetter.
108 pp. A Lesbian Gothic novel.   ISBN 0-930044-16-9   4.95

OUTLANDER by Jane Rule. 207 pp. Short stories and essays
by one of our finest writers.   ISBN 0-930044-17-7   6.95

ALL TRUE LOVERS by Sarah Aldridge. 292 pp. Romantic
novel set in the 1930s and 1940s.   ISBN 0-930044-10-X   7.95

A WOMAN APPEARED TO ME by Renee Vivien. 65 pp. A
classic; translated by Jeannette H. Foster.   ISBN 0-930044-06-1   5.00

CYTHEREA'S BREATH by Sarah Aldridge. 240 pp. Romantic
novel about women's entrance into medicine.
                                               ISBN 0-930044-02-9   6.95

TOTTIE by Sarah Aldridge. 181 pp. Lesbian romance in the
turmoil of the sixties.   ISBN 0-930044-01-0   6.95

THE LATECOMER by Sarah Aldridge. 107 pp. A delicate love
story.   ISBN 0-930044-00-2   5.00

ODD GIRL OUT by Ann Bannon.   ISBN 0-930044-83-5   5.95

I AM A WOMAN by Ann Bannon.   ISBN 0-930044-84-3   5.95

WOMEN IN THE SHADOWS by Ann Bannon.
                                               ISBN 0-930044-85-1   5.95

JOURNEY TO A WOMAN by Ann Bannon.
                                               ISBN 0-930044-86-X   5.95

BEEBO BRINKER by Ann Bannon.   ISBN 0-930044-87-8   5.95
     Legendary novels written in the fifties and sixties,
           set in the gay mecca of Greenwich Village.

VOLUTE BOOKS

JOURNEY TO FULFILLMENT   Early classics by Valerie   3.95
A WORLD WITHOUT MEN   Taylor: The Erika Frohmann   3.95
RETURN TO LESBOS   series.   3.95

These are just a few of the many Naiad Press titles — we are the oldest and
largest lesbian/feminist publishing company in the world. Please request a
complete catalog. We offer personal service; we encourage and welcome
direct mail orders from individuals who have limited access to bookstores
carrying our publications.